The Skorpion

on full-auto at the kayak

Seeing the line of holes appear along the vessel's prow, Bolan took advantage of the only move open to him: he snapped his hips violently sideways and dumped the canoe in an Eskimo roll.

The Executioner disappeared beneath the surface.

In the distance, Bjornstrom watched as Bolan's capsized craft was riddled by the Russian gunners.

With increasing speed the kayak shot toward the lip of the falls. For a dizzy moment it seemed to hang on the edge, then vanished into the maelstrom below.

For an instant the Icelander thought he saw the American's yellow helmet. Then it, too, dropped out of sight.

MACK BOLAN

The Executioner

DON PENDLETON's EXECUTIONER
MACK BOLAN
Blood Heat Zero

A GOLD EAGLE BOOK FROM
WORLDWIDE

TORONTO • NEW YORK • LONDON • PARIS
AMSTERDAM • STOCKHOLM • HAMBURG
ATHENS • MILAN • TOKYO • SYDNEY

First edition June 1986

ISBN 0-373-61090-4

Special thanks and acknowledgment to
Peter Leslie for his contributions to this work.

Printed in Canada

"Wouldst thou"—so the helmsman answered—
"Learn the secret of the sea?
Only those who brave its dangers
Comprehend its mystery!"
                    —Henry Wadsworth Longfellow

Every man, at some time in his life, needs
to find solace, to think, to plan, to search
for answers.
                    —Mack Bolan

THE
MACK BOLAN
LEGEND

Nothing less than a war could have fashioned the destiny of the man called Mack Bolan. Bolan earned the Executioner title in the jungle hellgrounds of Vietnam, for his skills as a crack sniper in pursuit of the enemy.

But this supreme soldier also wore another name—Sergeant Mercy. He was so tagged because of the compassion he showed to wounded comrades-in-arms and Vietnamese civilians.

Mack Bolan's second tour of duty ended prematurely when he was given emergency leave to return home and bury his family. Bolan made his peace at his parents' and sister's gravesite. Then he declared war on the evil force that had snatched his loved ones. The Mafia.

In a fiery one-man assault, he confronted the Mob head-on, carrying a cleansing flame to the urban menace. And when the battle smoke cleared, a solitary figure walked away alive.

He continued his lone-wolf struggle, and soon a hope of victory began to appear. But Mack Bolan had broken society's every rule. That same society started gunning for this elusive warrior—to no avail.

So Bolan was offered amnesty to work within the system against international terrorism. This time, as an official employee of Uncle Sam, Bolan wore yet another handle: Colonel John Phoenix. With government sanction now, and a command center at Stony Man Farm in Virginia's Blue Ridge Mountains, he and his new allies—Able Team and Phoenix Force—waged relentless war on a new adversary: the KGB and all it stood for.

Until the inevitable occurred. Bolan's one true love, the brilliant and beautiful April Rose, died at the hands of the Soviet terror machine.

Embittered and utterly saddened by this feral deed, Bolan broke the shackles of Establishment authority.

Now the big justice fighter is once more free to haunt the treacherous alleys of the shadow world.

Mack Bolan was leaving a Danish restaurant in Reykjavik, Iceland, when a second attempt was made on his life. The first had been less than two hours before, as he stood waiting for a taxi outside the Icelandair terminal at Keflavik airport, on a windswept peninsula jutting into the ocean twenty miles southwest of the capital.

Bolan had flown in from Copenhagen on a short-haul flight, the kind still known locally as "internal." The Executioner preferred to use the smaller airfields on his own time, as he was now, away from the rigors of his missions, from suspicious eyes.

Lately the warrior had felt increasingly that he needed some R and R to purge the mind, the spirit and, yeah, the body. He knew that battle fatigue could bring a weary soldier down. And Bolan's commitment to his duty, his destiny, had never been halfhearted in any way. In his present mode he might as well give up the fight and let the cannibals continue their savage march on gentle civilizers.

No damn way.

Mack Bolan knew the fight could wait, but for a short time, while a mentally exhausted warrior cleared his mind.

For a short time.

And this was why Bolan had decided on a self-imposed vacation in Iceland, on top of the world. In a way he felt on top of the world already, because the decision was made on his own, and not by any gentle prodding from allies like Hal Brognola.

In Iceland the environment was pure, Bolan felt, primitive. And a man could pit his strength, his wits, against the elements, become one with nature, making him whole again.

So the Executioner had chosen Keflavik airfield, rather than the big international airport nearer the city. These unimportant fields shared certain qualities that lent them an appearance of sameness—a few incoming and outgoing flights each day, a minimum of formalities and personnel who treated passengers like humans instead of cattle.

The atmosphere at these smaller airfields was casual and relaxed.

You could exchange banter with customs and immigration officials if you had a mind to. And you could get past them with a .44 AutoMag or a Beretta more easily than at Kennedy or Heathrow. Which was a plus if you were a hunted man like Mack Bolan.

And if you happened to be carrying, as he was that day, a 93-R and an AutoMag.

Although the Executioner had no intentions of using his two favorite handguns, he felt that it didn't make sense to take unnecessary chances, especially when one was involved in a trade such as Bolan's.

And that trade was Death.

After all, he *was* Mack Bolan.

In Iceland, Bolan planned to make a river excursion, from source to mouth.

The river was called the Jokulsa a Fjollum. In Icelandic, the name meant "glacier-fed stream in the mountains." Its source was deep beneath the mighty Vatnajokull ice cap that covered one-twelfth of the country's surface.

At first it was channeled through subterranean tunnels melted through the base of the glacier by geothermal heat generated from volcanoes that erupted beneath the ice. Then the river emerged into a desolate landscape of ancient lava flows and twisted northward into the Arctic Ocean through 130 miles of precipitous gorges punctuated by violent rapids and four major waterfalls.

The trip—effectively a coast-to-coast journey across the island—had been attempted once before, Bolan had read somewhere, by a twelve-man expedition using kayaks and inflatable rafts backed up by a snowmobile and a ULM, a gas-powered, delta-wing aircraft equipped with floats. It had taken them six weeks.

Bolan figured that if he cut the time by half and made the crossing alone in a single kayak, that would prove a sufficient test for his guts and his initiative. He would use an ULM only to ferry him from Egilsstadir, the nearest airfield, to the vast sinkhole in the ice that was the only entry to the source of the underground river.

Because he had to supervise the unloading of the crated ULM from the hold of the old 727 that had brought him from Denmark, and check out papers with the Icelandic customs, he had missed the airport bus that would have taken him to the city center. When he was through, he walked out of the superheated, cigar-smelling terminal and crossed a paved sidewalk toward the steel-and-glass canopy sheltering the taxi stand.

No cabs.

He looked around him. A veil of high-flying cirrus hid the sun. Below the barren promontory on which the airfield was located, gray waves crumbled into dirty white foam as the wind whipped the surface of the sea. On the far side of the inlet, he could see the snowcapped mountains behind Reykjavik.

Behind him, there was one vehicle in the parking lot—a dark blue Ford into which the customs and immigration officers were climbing. The vehicle bumped across the lot, turned through the gates and took the highway leading to Reykjavik. He went back into the terminal.

There was no one around. A group of geology students who had been on the plane had taken the bus into the city. The 727 had left on the last leg of its flight to Scotland, carrying with it the few transit passengers who had been thronging the duty-free store in search of cheap whiskey and Brennavin, the pungent Icelandic liquor. Through the PA speakers a lone unaccompanied alto saxophone lamented the loneliness of man.

But the ticket counter with its stack of blank forms was deserted, unlocked doors to the empty administration offices stood open, a steel grill blocked off the bar. The next plane was not due until dusk, and the airport personnel had gone back to town.

Bolan walked unchallenged past the immigration desk into the departure lounge. Through wide glass windows he stared at two Cessna executive jets parked on the apron. In the distance a lighthouse on the tip of the headland pointed a single finger at the cold sky.

Nearer, a tractor towing a string of baggage trailers trundled through the open doors of a maintenance hangar. A man in white coveralls rolled shut the hangar doors and left the field as deserted as the terminal.

Beyond the perimeter, a chain link fence enclosed a group of low yellow buildings marking the site of the U.S. naval base built during the American occupation of Iceland in World War II. The technicians stationed there now under a NATO agreement were part of a high-tech unit whose job was to monitor the movements toward the North Atlantic of Russian warships, nuclear submarines, trawlers and the huge fishing-factory ships that so often themselves were no more than covers for sophisticated electronic surveillance equipment.

Bolan hoped there were not too many spooks on detail there. He was, he knew, on the hit list not only of foreign agencies such as the KGB, the SDEC, and Britain's MI-6 but also of the CIA and the National Security Agency. It would sure cramp his style if any one of those guys knew he was in Iceland—even if it was for a vacation.

He turned back into the waiting room. It still smelled of cigar smoke and stale coffee. There was a copy of the country's biggest daily newspaper lying open on a bench. He picked it up and turned to the classified section. He found what he wanted on the second page— an advertisement for a taxi service in the city. He went to a pay phone, dropped in a coin and dialed the number.

Half an hour, they told him. He returned to the lounge. The high, flat, vibratoless cadences of the taped alto explored a scale somewhere up among the stars. Out on the apron the stressed metal skin of the Cessnas was shivering in the wind.

Bolan was waiting outside the terminal ten minutes before his cab was due. He blew into his cupped hands, hunched against the icy breeze. To his surprise he saw the cab turning into the airport entrance almost at once. The vehicle—a Mercedes sedan with the light behind the for-hire sign extinguished—swung around and headed for the taxi stand.

Bolan picked up his luggage, stepped out into the roadway and waited for the car to stop.

Instead the big sedan picked up speed as the driver slammed the lever into second and floored the pedal. The engine screamed as the wide Mercedes leaped for Bolan.

Only the Executioner's seasoned nerves, razor sharp through half a lifetime of combat in the world's hot spots, saved him from the hurtling vehicle. In the hundredth of a second's advantage given to him as the danger signal flashed from eyes to brain to muscles, he threw himself violently backward into the shelter.

The driver wrenched the wheel as Bolan fell. The Mercedes slewed sideways on the pavement, and the front fender missed him by a fraction of an inch as it plowed into a steel support halfway along the shelter. The support buckled and split; the shelter erupted in a fountain of glass and splintered wood.

Tires squealed. The sedan broadsided half across the roadway, snaked and then righted itself. Bolan was shouldering his way up and out of the wreckage, the Beretta in his right hand. He fired, shook glass fragments from his hair and fired again—a three-shot group that starred the rear window of the Mercedes.

Once more the big car swerved. Then the exhausts bellowed and it powered toward the highway. Evidently the killers were not armed...or they didn't expect their intended victim to be toting iron and preferred not to trade shots with a professional.

Soon after, the taxi that Bolan had ordered arrived.

On the way into town he scarcely noticed the bleak, treeless coastline, the vivid green mosses that covered the black lava soil of the lowlands. Too many questions were jockeying for position in his mind. Who were the would-be assassins? Why here, of all places, would anyone want to take him out?

He wasn't on any kind of mission; it wasn't even a recon trip. He'd never been to Iceland before. It was less than forty-eight hours since he had made up his mind, reserved his ticket and hired the kayak and the ULM.

Yet someone knew he was coming—and they didn't like it.

If they hadn't known, he must have been recognized at the airport and hasty plans made to dispose of him.

In either case, one thing was clear—whoever it was must believe that he *was* on a mission, some kind of search-and-destroy operation.

It followed that there were facts to find out, incriminating facts important enough to risk murder to keep quiet.

Some person or persons unknown had something going that the Executioner—if he had really been working on it—could have loused up. What could it be? Drugs? Prostitution? Some kind of Mafia racket? Unlikely. A terrorist plot then?

In *Iceland*? He dismissed the thought.

Someone had done their best to eliminate him nevertheless. Of the two possibilities, he favored the second—that he had by chance been recognized at the airport and the wrong conclusion drawn. The attempt to run him down showed all the signs of a hasty, spur-of-the-moment plan. Otherwise, if they knew anything about him, they would have been armed.

Bolan shrugged as he stared at the white houses with their multicolored roofs on the outskirts of Reykjavik. Okay, someone carrying a load of guilt was prepared to kill to protect his investment. But what the hell—it had nothing to do with him; he was on vacation, dammit. The heat would presumably be off once they realized he was not on their trail.

That was before the second attempt.

Bolan planned to play the tourist for two days in Reykjavik. He would see enough of the Icelandic countryside on his self-imposed river trip. The kayak and the ULM were to be freighted to Egilsstadir, on the east coast of the island, and he would follow on a domestic flight two days later.

Right now he was tired and he was hungry. He checked into the Hotel Wotan, in the city center. It was a comfortable, old-fashioned place with creaking elevators and its central heating and hot water drawn—as it was for every dwelling in Reykjavik—from the thermal springs whose source Bolan himself would soon be exploring.

His third-floor room overlooked Austurvollur Square and the red-brick, steep-roofed Althing building where the parliament met. After a shave and a shower he went out to eat and take in the nightlife of the city—though in this season nightlife was something of a misnomer—it was weeks before the winter "darkening time," when the earth's Northern Hemisphere tilted away from the sun and the hours of darkness grew unbearably long, the incidence of alcoholism increased and the murder rate shot up.

Bolan almost smiled as he thought of his narrow escape earlier. These people were getting ahead of themselves.

He arrived at Nielsen's, which was recommended by the hotel's head porter. It was a candlelit basement and the meal—smorrebrod preceded by slices of smoked sturgeon followed by raw herring in a variety of sauces—was excellent. Thule, the Icelandic beer, was practically nonalcoholic, but the aquavit aperitif was strong and the after-dinner Brennivin more fiery still. It was with a feeling of well-being but with combat instincts on alert that Bolan climbed the stone steps beneath the striped awning to regain the street.

His veteran's sixth sense saved him again. The gun was equipped with a sound suppressor, and there was a flash hider over the muzzle. But something indefinable in the gloom—a darker patch of shadow that moved, a tiny scrape of metal, a rolled-down auto window that snared a gleam of light from a distant street lamp—warned him of danger. He shoved the doorman violently down the steps and dropped to the sidewalk in a single fluid motion.

The *phut* of the gun was barely audible. The metal-jacketed death bringer spanged off the restaurant-area railings behind Bolan's head and screeched into the sky. The second shot flattened itself against the brickwork at the top of the steps, at the height Bolan's chest would have been an instant before.

Then a bus rumbled down the street with a string of cars behind it. A truck laden with barrels passed in the other direction. By the time the street was clear again, Bolan was facedown along the slant of the stairway, elbows resting on the sidewalk, the Beretta cradled in his two hands.

He held his breath, scanning the line of parked cars on the far side of the roadway. He figured the shots came from one of them. Or maybe from a marksman standing between two of the vehicles. Or even someone hidden in a doorway on the opposite sidewalk.

Bolan's ice-chip eyes raked the target area.

"What the hell's going on?" the doorman's angry voice protested from below. "You can't—"

"Crazy fool with a gun," the Executioner whispered. "Keep quiet and stay where you are."

"You're the one's that's crazy! Let me call the pol—"

"No! Let me handle it."

Bolan's voice was not much louder than a whisper, but it was enough to pinpoint his position for the hidden gunman. The silenced weapon coughed three more times. Bolan ducked below the top step as the slugs gouged chips from the flagstones paving the sidewalk.

But this time he had a line on the enemy position.

Among the parked vehicles, four were immediately opposite Nielsen's frontage—a Volvo station wagon, a Citroën, a panel truck and a Swedish Saab sedan. Bolan had at first suspected the truck—maybe an opening concealed in the lettering along its side—but as soon as he scanned the row he saw that he was mistaken. In the half light, reflected illumination from the far street lamp gleamed dully on paintwork and veneered the windows of the parked vehicles.

Except for the window above the driver's door on the Saab. Instead of the faint sheen of glass, here there was simply an empty space.

No one would leave the driver's window of a parked car open on a chilly evening like this.

As Bolan watched, his suspicions were confirmed. A black shape materialized in the open space above the door. Its outline was definitive. An ambusher popping up for a snap shot before he dropped back out of sight and out of range.

Bolan was ready. He fired first. His Beretta was equipped with a suppressor. A sharp cry came from the other side of the street and the silhouette vanished.

A red light at an intersection two hundred yards away changed to green. Traffic surged forward. The Executioner was on his feet, dodging for cover behind a cruising taxi, racing for the far side of the roadway. He flung himself down between the Volvo and the Citroën. It was too dangerous to approach the Saab without checking first. He might only have winged his assailant; the guy could be playing possum, waiting to get in a close-up sucker shot as Bolan approached; there might even be two of them.

There were.

Fragments of stone stung Bolan's face as a hail of slugs hosed down beneath the Citroën and into the space between the two cars. Heavy-caliber shells flattened themselves against the pavement, bounced up against exhausts and the underside of the engines and whined away into the shadows. The second gunman was aiming to score with a ricochet if he couldn't make a direct hit.

Bolan considered his arsenal situation. He had refilled the Beretta's clip in his hotel room—there were still fourteen rounds left in the box magazine. He was also carrying the big silver AutoMag, but the heavy cannon was unsilenced and he didn't want to draw too much attention to this private battle.

But there was only one way to finish it quickly.

Attack! He waited until the stoplights released another parcel of traffic, then he used the noise of the passing vehicles to mask his own movements, bellying his way beneath the Citroën until he was looking out at the grille of the panel truck. The shooting from the Saab behind it had stopped. Bolan sprang upright by the truck fender and dashed, not across the sidewalk into the shelter of a doorway, but out into the open, in the center of the roadway.

The second killer, on his feet beside the Swedish sedan, with his gun questing left and right in search of his target, was taken completely by surprise. He whirled, the Executioner's menacing figure registered on his peripheral vision. Too late.

Bolan triggered the 93-R, a 3-shot burst. The 9 mm parabellums drilled through the hardman's forehead. Bolan saw a momentary cloud of crimson in the diffuse light, as the gunner's skull disintegrated. Then he dropped into forever, hidden from sight behind the Saab's hood.

Bolan ran to the car's front window. His first shot had scored. The man who had opened fire was dead, too, his faceless body sprawled over the blood-spattered seat.

At first glance there was nothing on either of them to show who they were or who had sent them. Bolan could not wait for a second glance. Although the exchange had been virtually noiseless, passersby had already gathered at the traffic lights. Several cars had stopped. Across the road the doorman was shouting and there was a wail of sirens in the distance.

Bolan crossed the sidewalk in two quick strides and melted into the shadows of an alleyway. The last thing he wanted was an interview with the members of Iceland's police. They would ask too many questions, study his ID, maybe check him out with Interpol. There was not much crime in Iceland—foreigners who broke the law were not welcome. The interview could turn into an interrogation.

And however much Bolan had been the injured party on this occasion, the fact remained that his Interpol dossier had him listed as an outlaw...and he had killed two men on a Reykjavik street.

If he quietly vanished, with luck, he would get away unrecognized.

There were no witnesses to the shooting or to the clumsy attempt on his life at the airport; the doorman was the only person who had actually seen him during the firefight; he had made no reservation and left no name at the restaurant.

He releathered the Beretta and found his way back to the Hotel Wotan by a roundabout route. Thirty minutes later he was in bed.

He had barely fallen asleep when his unknown enemies struck again.

2

The attack was stealthier than the first two. If Bolan had not been a superlight sleeper, his warrior instincts sensitive to the slightest deviation from the norm—and if he had not already been alerted by the two previous attempts—the intrusion could have passed unnoticed.

For one thing, the clandestine entry was not made the obvious way—via the fire escape, the balcony and the floor-length double-casement windows, which would have presented no problem to a professional. A small lobby, with closets on one side and the bathroom on the other, separated the bedroom from the door to the hallway. And it was through this door, the lock oiled with an aerosol spray and a skeleton key expertly maneuvered, that the killer came in.

The entry was completely noiseless. It was perhaps some infinitesimal alteration in the atmospheric pressure, an exhalation of breath felt rather than heard, that brought the Executioner instantly awake, every nerve tingling with anticipation, his whole body tense as a coiled spring.

He held his breath.

No shape passed across the strip of half light showing between the drapes. No current of air fanned his face. No board creaked. Bolan's right hand slipped beneath the pillows; his fingers curled around the butt of the Beretta.

A brilliant light blinded him; a high-intensity beam that shafted from a powerful electric torch at the foot of the bed. Clutching the gun, he rolled violently to one side.

That was when the second intruder struck.

A flurry of movement from behind. A heavy body leaped, pinning him to the bed. Hard knees crushed his shoulders, a muscular leg trapped his gun hand before he could withdraw it from beneath the covers.

The flashlight advanced. The knees clamped vicelike on either side of his head, pinning him. Bolan heaved, threshing desperately from side to side. But the man with the light was now kneeling on his hips, immobilizing his body, too.

A hand with an iron grip closed over his jaw, fingers on one side, thumb on the other, forcing open his mouth. The end of a plastic funnel was jammed between his teeth.

Bolan bucked and writhed more violently still, but the combined weight of his assailants held him down. There was a gurgle of liquid.

He gagged as it rushed through the funnel, flooding his mouth and throat. A second hand squeezed shut his nostrils. For one of the few times in his life he was entirely helpless—he had to swallow the fluid or suffocate. There was no other choice.

He swallowed.

Fierce heat fired the membranes of his gullet. He experienced an instant of panic when he feared they were forcing him to drink some caustic acid. Then came realization... and with it complete bewilderment.

He was drinking cognac.

Relief, temporary though it was, automatically relaxed his taut muscles. His body went limp. Fractionally, perhaps without acting consciously, the attackers also relinquished a small percentage of their hold.

It was then that Bolan saw the light glinting on the hypodermic syringe.

And the killer straddling his hips made his first—and fatal—mistake.

Bolan was still swallowing brandy, gasping for breath between each swirl of the fiery liquor. The man with the syringe shuffled himself up from Bolan's hips until his knees were thrusting against the Executioner's armpits. His captor raised the syringe, directing the flashlight downward with his other hand.

But although his arms were still pinioned by the first man, Bolan's legs were now free of the killer's weight.

Galvanized into action, he kicked away the covers, brought up his legs and scissored his ankles around the guy's head. He jerked his legs savagely down onto the bed again, knocking the intruder with the syringe backward. The hood's own legs shot upward, knocking the man who was kneeling on Bolan's shoulders off balance.

The funnel fell from the Executioner's mouth. Cognac splashed over the sheets as the bottle spun from the attacker's grasp. The beam from the flashlight swung crazily across the ceiling.

For the moment there was a frenzied tangle of limbs on the alcohol-soaked bed. Then Bolan had thrown off the two intruders and was crouched by the night table, ready to spring. He feinted toward the first hood, who was still sprawled on the pillows with the gun beneath him...and then swung violently the other way.

He seized the hypodermic, tore it from the hardman's grasp and plunged the needle with lightning speed into the guy's left eye, ramming the syringe home with the heel of his hand.

The deadly point punctured the eyeball, pierced the cortex and penetrated the cerebellum. The hardman cried out once and fell, clawing at his face. He twitched and then lay still.

Bolan was already on the other guy. They rolled from the bed to the floor. Anger and surprise—and perhaps some extra stimulation from the liquor he had been forced to swallow—lent Bolan a manic strength. His powerful shoulder muscles rippled as he heaved the attacker facedown onto the bed. An instant later he was kneeling on the guy's calves, hauling the top half of his body upright and jamming a forearm across his windpipe and beneath his chin at the same time.

The hood writhed, choking. The point of his elbow rammed backward into the Executioner's solar plexus, but Bolan held on grimly. A hand scrabbled for the soldier's groin. He slammed his hips against the killer's buttocks. And now the palm of his free hand was cradling the back of his victim's head. Sweating, he exerted pressure.

On the rumpled bed, their distorted shadows thrown across wall and ceiling by the flashlight, which had rolled to the far corner of the room, the two men remained locked in motionless, almost noiseless, combat. Only their harsh breathing, an occasional creak from the bedsprings as one or the other minimally shifted position, a barely discernible click from tortured sinew or tendon, broke the silence.

Beads of moisture stood out on Bolan's forehead. His opponent's breathing grew more labored and hoarse as the pressure on windpipe and neck inexorably increased; his struggles weakened.

And then abruptly Bolan summoned a supreme effort— an upward jerk of the forearm coupled with a sudden titanic thrust with the palm of the other hand. A dull crack echoed in the room.

The hood's body went limp in Bolan's grasp. He allowed it to slide to the floor.

He clambered off the bed, breathing heavily, and examined the two bodies. Both men had been rough, muscular, evidently hard living. But that was about all he could deduce. They could have come from anywhere in the northern half of Europe. A search of their clothes yielded nothing. They were wearing anonymous gray combat fatigues. No labels, no insignia, no papers in the empty pockets.

Certain things, however, were clearer to Bolan now.

Like the planned scenario for this nighttime visit.

Gingerly he extracted the hypodermic syringe from the first attacker's eye socket. Over the hand basin in the bathroom, he examined the contents, squirted out a second sample. The almond odor was enough to convince him.

A derivative of prussic acid. Muscular contractions followed by immediate cardiac arrest.

By the time the hotel staff realized that the occupant of room 321 wasn't going to require any breakfast—probably not until noon the following day—the muscles would be relaxed, the poison itself would have been dissipated. Symptoms, therefore, of a classic heart attack.

Bolan could follow the reasoning imposed on the police. A killer in town, a man wanted by every security agency in the Western world. He drinks too much, in a local restaurant. Afterward he runs amok in the street, kills two innocent bystanders and then goes back to his hotel and drinks himself to sleep. A massive coronary following such excesses would be a believable sequel. Alerted by the remaining fumes of brandy, stronger and more distinctive than aquavit or Brennivin, the police surgeon and the autopsy doctor would look no further. Very neat.

There were two other conclusions that Bolan could draw from the night's events.

One, whatever it was that the hoods' boss or bosses were trying so hard to keep under wraps must be very important indeed—important enough to mount a team operation that had already cost them four soldiers, even if Bolan hadn't winged a fifth in the Mercedes at the airport.

Two, it must be the kind of thing that those bosses, knowing Bolan, would expect him to be interested in destroying.

That narrowed the field some, but it still wasn't exactly specific.

The Executioner was intrigued. What could be going on in Iceland that the bad boys thought he had been sent to stamp out?

Just to satisfy his curiosity—and because he was becoming goddamned tired of these continual attempts on his life—he determined to do his best to find out.

He wasn't necessarily going to do anything about it when he had found out. Unless, of course, it was the kind of thing...but it would wait until he knew more.

Meanwhile, before he continued his vacation, he would offer himself, knowingly this time, as a decoy. Maybe if he could get close enough to talk, he could convince them that he was not interested at all in their conspiracy, whatever it was.

But first, there were two bodies to dispose of—in some way that would leave no finger pointing in his direction. The police, especially after the fray outside Nielsen's, were the last people he wished to complain to, explain to or wise up to the unsuccessful attempts on his life. He would handle that one himself.

The guy with the broken neck was not too difficult. He was a burglar, wasn't he? There were skeleton keys in his pocket to prove it—or there would be as soon as Bolan had removed them from the lock of his door. Too bad the guy missed his footing and fell to his death in the area from a third-floor balcony.

Bolan opened the double-glazed windows, heaved the body onto his shoulder and stepped out into the cold pre-dawn light. Bending over the balcony rail, he lowered the corpse to the full extent of his arms, swung it left, right, left again . . . and then, gasping with the effort, relaxed his grip and let the corpse sail away to one side and down.

The inert body landed below the balcony of the next-door room with a thump and a clatter that seemed to the Executioner as loud as a peal of thunder in a tropical storm. But no window in the hotel facade was thrown open; no questing heads and shoulders appeared; no angry voice shouted. After a minute he went back into his room and drew the drapes. Let the cops work out why a man with skeleton keys that would open doors inside the building should have fallen from a balcony outside it.

The second body posed more of a problem. With a bloody hole where one eye should have been, it would be difficult trying to pass that one off as accidental death.

Soft footed and in his trousers now, Bolan prowled the corridors until he found what he wanted—a small room beyond the elevators and the stairwell, where the hotel service personnel stored bed linen and cleaning materials. A sliding panel on one wall opened onto a laundry chute. He dragged the body along the passageway and stuffed it headfirst down the chute.

If it slid freely the whole way to the basement, there would at first be no way of telling which floor it came from; if it became jammed someplace . . . well, with luck the chambermaids would not change the bed linen in vacated rooms much before ten-thirty. And Bolan would be long gone before they discovered the chute was blocked.

He returned to his room, wiped the attackers' fingerprints from door handles and anything else the attackers might have touched, and then washed out the syringe and threw it down toward the body in the area.

By eight o'clock he had checked out. Ten minutes later he was on the far side of the square, mending an enforced cognac hangover with strong black coffee in the breakfast room of the Hotel Thor. At nine-fifteen he arranged to rent a car with the help of the clerk behind the information desk at the Hotel Loftleider, half a dozen blocks away.

3

Bolan rented a four-wheel-drive Mitsubishi Colt Shogun. He chose the tough Japanese off-roader for two reasons: first, because he intended to drive a fair distance and he had heard that only the main Icelandic coastal route was paved—most of the inland roads being at best surfaced with packed gravel—and secondly because he wanted his planned showdown to be in an area so remote that even the dirt roads might not reach it.

Only then, Bolan felt, would he have the opportunity to bring them clear out into the open, confront them, and . . . yeah, make the bastards sing! Maybe then, depending on their answers, he could convince them that he wasn't in the country on their account.

Unless he discovered they were into some nefarious activity that his conscience wouldn't let him leave be. But that was something he could worry about after they talked. Right now the priority was to move.

He slung his luggage in back of the tall, compact Colt utility, filled up with gasoline and took the road north from Reykjavik.

He intended—he told the young woman at the rental agency, just in case anyone was checking on him—to take in the huge aluminum plant that was Iceland's only heavy industry and then follow the coast road as far as the port of Bogarnes. After that he would drive inland along the fertile Nodura Valley.

On the pretense of asking her advice, he contrived also to let her know that afterward he wanted to cross the bare central plateau, detour as far as the picturesque fringe of the Langjokull glacier and then head for Akureyri on the north coast. This was the country's second largest port, a few miles only from the Arctic Circle, and apart from the variety of Norwegian, Danish, Russian and Swedish shipping docked there, he could also visit the great Laxa hydroelectric complex.

This ultramodern super-power-station, thirty-five percent owned by Iceland's National Energy Authority, would be a natural draw for any engineer, as Bolan had told her he was.

The coast road was impressive, following the rugged cliff contours above a steel-gray sea. The sky was a pale cloudless blue, and it was quite warm. At any other time, Bolan would have relaxed, enjoying the unfamiliar scenery. But today it was the Shogun's wide-angle rearview mirror that claimed all the attention he could spare from the winding road ahead.

By American or European mainland standards, traffic was light. But there was a fairly continuous procession of cars, fruit and vegetable delivery trucks, and occasional buses traveling in each direction. Most of the vehicles were sturdy, Northern European makes—Volkswagen, Mercedes, Audi, Swedish Volvos and Saabs—which made it tough singling out any potential tail—everything looked much the same. It was not until noon, after he had suffered a conducted tour over the aluminum works and strolled the many-masted, herring-scented quays of Bogarnes, that Bolan was able to even suspect a possible tail.

A scarlet, diesel-powered Mercedes 300-GD—a high-built, 4 x 4 utility not unlike the machine he was piloting—had tucked in behind him some way south of the port. He had lost it in the narrow streets of the Old Town. But when, after his walk half an hour later, he took the right-hand turn for Desey and the headwaters of the Nodura, the red off-roader was there again. So was an Audi Quattro he had first noticed on the outskirts of Bogarnes and a Volkswagen Passat station wagon.

He lost the VW at Hvammur, but the other two kept position behind him, first one and then the other surfacing in the decreasing stream of traffic that lined up behind the Shogun and then passed.

Bolan was practically certain now . . . and then, when he made another right turn somewhere beyond a small town called Fornilvammer, hoping to find a trail that would take him near the glacier, he discovered that he was on his own.

For as far as he could see in the curved mirror, the narrow track unrolled emptily behind him across the bleak, treeless land.

The pursuers—if pursuers they had been—had given up.

Ten miles farther on he discovered why.

The trail petered out, while the ice cap was still no more than a shimmering line in the distance, in a rocky wilderness that had once been a lava flow—a deserted plateau that was bare of vegetation and littered with shallow lakes. There was no turnout, no intersection, no alternative route; there was nothing to do but turn around and go back.

If either of those cars *was* following him, all they would have had to do would be to park near the original turnout and wait for him to come back.

And that was what they did.

After that they made no pretense that they just happened to be following the same route; they fell in behind the Colt, first the Audi, then the Merc G-Wagen, with a precision that was almost military, maintaining their exact distance at whatever speed the Executioner chose.

Bolan had a sudden disturbing thought. Could they in fact *be* military? Or at any rate the equivalent?

Iceland had no army, no navy, no air force, and only a small coast-guard service. Even the police numbered less than six hundred country-wide. But there could be some kind of security organization. Had his outlaw status somehow been flashed ahead of his arrival? Were they keeping tabs on him to see what the hell he was up to in their country? Had they connected him with the bodies at the hotel?

Unlikely. In that case surely they would simply have taken him in.

But there was also the possibility that one of the attempts on his life had been reported; maybe the authorities were checking him out, curious to know why he had not complained.

More likely still was the simplest explanation—the goons on his tail were from the same outfit that had fouled up the earlier attempts on his life. If that was the case, it suited the Executioner fine; that was just the way he wanted it.

Once they had been maneuvered into a position where he could gain the upper hand, he figured he would at least have a chance to find out what the hell went on.

Bolan made few mistakes in his tactical appreciations. This was one of them.

He led the procession toward Poroddsstadir and the long, narrow sea arm known as Hruta Fjord. Then near the village of Stathur, when the steely headwaters of the craggy twenty-five-mile inlet were already visible below the left-hand margin of the road, he veered away to the east, bumping over a stony track that spiraled up into the Vistur Hunavatns highlands.

The G-Wagen and the Audi followed, closing now.

Bolan accelerated, wheels spinning clouds of dust into the mountain air as he hurled the Colt around each curve.

Breasting the final rise, he jammed momentarily on the brake pedal. Ahead, the trail looped crazily down the face of an escarpment and then lost itself in a confusion of giant boulders far below. Beyond these scattered segments of rock a bare landscape stretched away in gentle undulations toward a line of ancient volcanic cones.

Bolan maneuvered the utility down the grade, zigzagging the rock face, showering stones and loose stone chips into the void at each twist in the track. He wrenched the off-roader between the boulders at the foot of the cliff and steered out across a plain floored with coarse upland grass.

Two hundred yards behind, the G-Wagen bumped out from the dark and ragged outcrops in pursuit. But the rough ground proved too much for the Audi. With a lower ground clearance, the powerful sedan tore the casing from its rear differential on a rocky projection and ground to a halt with a scream of ruptured metal.

Bolan grinned.

There was no doubt now that the followers—two stalled in the Audi and three in the Merc, as far as he could see—were out to get him.

Three hundred yards out from the escarpment, granules of toughened glass stung the back of the Executioner's neck as the rear window of the Colt exploded inward. Someone in the Mercedes had opened fire with an SMG or a machine pistol. Heavy slugs ripped through the fiberglass top and punched holes in the steel bodywork of the vehicle.

But the range was too great for accurate shooting, and in any case the grass, smooth enough from a distance, was in fact so pitted with small hollows, so studded with hummocks that no marksman could hope to score from a bouncing utility traveling at more than forty mph.

Bolan gunned the 4 x 4. Some way beyond a slight swell in the treeless surface of the plain he had seen a slash of brighter, more vivid green coloring the dun landscape. His plan, a sudden decision, depended on his ability to dip out of sight of the Mercedes for an instant before he approached that stretch of green.

A prehistoric stone monument stood on the crest of the rise. Three vast rock columns, topped by two equally heavy horizontal slabs, hid the Colt momentarily from view as Bolan swerved sideways and threw out his luggage. Then he was rocketing down the far slope toward that bright green space.

And briefly, but for long enough, the pursuers dropped out of sight on the far side of the low ridge.

Bolan braked fiercely, opened the driver's door and dived out of the decelerating Shogun. He hit the ground, shoulder-rolled and came up crouching, sprinting for the shelter of a solitary rock that pierced the grassy slope.

The off-roader, picking up speed again, plowed on with its engine bellowing. A twenty-pound stone, harvested by Bolan in case of emergencies during his fruitless attempt to make the Langjokull glacier, weighted its acceleration pedal flat to the floorboards.

As the G-Wagen appeared over the crest, Bolan's mount was hitting the half century. Swaying giddily from side to side, it made the foot of the slope, shot up a small ramp and took to the air for more than twenty feet before it hit the jade-green surface of the brighter area.

The Colt didn't bounce. The green surface erupted. The utility, obscured by a curtain of color, appeared to be half engulfed. Slowly it began sinking from sight.

The flat green swath was no grassy upland meadow but a treacherous quagmire, one of the deadly bogs for which the interior of Iceland was notorious.

The Mercedes squealed to a halt on the fringe of the morass. Three men, unaware of Bolan's escape, got out. A driver and two gunners, as he had surmised. He was ready behind the rocky outcrop with Big Thunder, the stainless-steel .44 AutoMag in his right hand.

He felt no compunction. These guys—or soldiers from the same outfit—had three times tried to take him out.

The driver stayed by the door of the G-Wagen. The two hardmen—armed, Bolan saw, with Uzi submachine guns—walked warily to the shelving demarcation line between the grass and the moss-green slime of the swamp. With trigger fingers at the ready, they eyed the slowly submerging Colt, waiting for its occupant to make some desperate attempt to escape.

Nobody emerged. The abandoned utility was already more than halfway under. As they watched, the obscene mass flowed in through the open door and began to fill the cab.

"Over here!" Bolan called from his hiding place.

The killers whirled, flame blossoming from the stubby muzzles of their Uzis. A hail of lead flailed against the rock, shrieking into the sky as the multiple detonations lost themselves in space.

Bolan had hurled himself sideways. He fired two-handed, stitching a classic left-right-left figure eight across the bodies of the two hoods.

One died on his feet, with white splinters of bone pricking through the crimson ruin of his chest. The other, caught in the left shoulder, spun away, hurled backward over the morass by the demon impact of a heavy Magnum flesh-shredder. He splashed into the wicked slime...and fatally, instead of lying flat or trying to roll himself to the side, he panicked and struck out, some crazed instinct prompting him to head away from the gunfire, toward the sinking Colt.

Bolan could do nothing but watch him die. But before that he had wasted the driver of the Merc with a 3-shot burst that shattered the near window and let daylight into the killer's skull before he could free his Police Special from its shoulder holster.

The wounded assassin was quickly sucked under. His screaming face gurgled beneath the heaving slime; the last corner of the Shogun's roof squelched out of sight.

Bolan stood and went to examine the bodies.

Zero.

Negative as the corpses in the hotel room in Reykjavik— gray coveralls with no labels, no identifying marks; no papers, no documents, not even a wallet. The one undamaged face was neither Oriental, middle eastern nor Mediterranean in type. Like the others it could have come from any country in Northern Europe.

The Executioner sighed. He reloaded the AutoMag, climbed into the G-Wagen and fired the engine. He drove back toward the wrecked Audi, stopping on the way to recover his luggage from behind the stone monument. A hell of a way civilization had come since they were erected, he thought bitterly.

Bolan hoped the other stranded gunmen—seeing the red utility return—would assume their prey had been eliminated in the firefight and their comrades were on the way back to report success.

But it was too much to hope for.

Maybe they could see that there was only one rider instead of three; maybe there was some signal he should have given. In any event they opened fire while the G-Wagen was still more than one hundred yards away.

That was their first mistake.

The range, again, was too great for the handguns they were using. They must have concentrated all the heavier stuff they had on the spearhead detail in the Merc. That was the second.

Their third mistake, fatal in any warlike encounter, was to underestimate the strength and determination of their opponent.

Bolan made no attempt to slacken speed, take evasive action or duck out of the fight. He drove the heavy Mercedes utility straight at the sedan, keeping an iron grip on the bucking wheel with one hand, pumping lethal .44 boattails from the AutoMag with the other hand.

The two-man crew from the Audi Quattro was out of the car and behind the hood before the Mercedes made half the distance, spitting death from revolvers he guessed to be Police Specials, like the dead driver's. But the relatively lightweight .38s were no match for the steel-drilling, 240-grain messengers of death thundering from the Executioner's cannon. After a few snap shots the goons dropped from sight, obviously waiting for him to exhaust his magazine.

The Merc's windshield was holed in two places; the laminated glass starred but held. Apart from the last of a rear window there was, so far as Bolan could see, no other damage. He braced himself for the shock, steering the G-Wagen hard at the Audi's rear quarter.

The massive iron grille protecting the utility's front smashed into the sedan's rear wheel and trunk, mangling the bodywork and rupturing the fuel tank. Gasoline splashed out as the Audi tipped over onto its side with a screech of crumpled steel.

Bolan rocked the G-Wagen to a halt and leaped down behind one of the boulders. Big Thunder's magazine was empty but now he held the Beretta 93-R in his hand. Folding down the forward hand grip, he sighted carefully and loosed off a single shot.

The slug was well aimed, striking the rock on which the Audi had foundered at a shallow angle and ricocheting away in a shower of sparks. The inflammable vapor rising from the savaged fuel tank ignited with a dull thump. An instant later the gasoline remaining in the tank exploded, transforming the capsized Audi into a blazing fireball. From beneath the boiling, black-tinged maelstrom a scarecrow figure erupted, beating ineffectually at its flaming clothes with charred hands.

Bolan fired a mercy round to terminate the hood's agony.

The last man—the one the Executioner was determined to keep alive—dashed out from behind the holocaust and headed for a rock shelf, firing from the hip as he ran.

Bolan dropped him in midstride with an auto 3-shot aimed low. The hardman's gun skittered from his hands as he dropped, writhing, with shattered knees.

Bolan ran across and hauled the guy to his feet, one big hand bunched in the anonymous gray coveralls. "Okay, hotshot," he snarled, "time to start talking, now!" He shook the injured gunman fiercely in his grasp.

The man's eyes, almost colorless, showed neither fear nor hate nor even shock. His face was expressionless; only the teeth sunk into his lower lip revealed the effort he was making not to scream aloud at the pain scything his splintered kneecaps.

Bolan jammed the Beretta's muzzle against the man's forehead, let him see the trigger finger whitening in the squeeze.

"Who the hell are you?" the Executioner grated. "Who sent you? And why are you trying to kill me?"

The wounded killer choked. His hand flew to his mouth.

Suddenly he smiled up into the big guy's face.

And shuddered.

Bolan realized too late that this was no involuntary hand gesture provoked by a spasm of agony, no expression of humor, however grim.

The lips were drawn back from discolored teeth by a fearful rictus. The body stiffened and then went limp. The head flopped forward and an acrid almond odor caused Bolan to release his grip in a reflex of horror.

The guy had bitten on a cyanide pill rather than talk.

Bolan released his breath in a long sigh of frustration.

"Damn!" he said forcefully.

His ruse to decoy the assassins out into the open had worked exactly the way he had planned it.

And he had ended up as he started . . . knowing precisely nothing.

What now?

He shrugged. The car-rental agency would be surprised when he turned in a 300-GD off-roader that was worth five thousand bucks more than the Colt he had hired—even if the Mercedes needed a certain amount of attention to the rear window and windshield. But once he had handled that little problem, he decided, he would continue with his vacation as planned.

And if the mysterious organization that seemed so anxious to waste him followed him down below the ice cap . . . well, he'd tackle that one when it happened.

He returned to the G-Wagen and headed for the trail that wound back up the escarpment.

4

A Russian factory ship loomed above the trawlers and tugs berthed along the waterfront at Akureyri. "Loaded to the gunwales with surveillance equipment," the man wearing the watch cap said to Bolan. "We know it, and they know we know it, but nobody does nothing about it."

"That so?" the Executioner said casually.

"No trawlermen aboard that ship." The sailor spit into the sawdust at his feet. "Soviet navy specialists, most of 'em. They take our fish and louse up the goddam breeding grounds, but mainly they use those boats to keep tabs on shipping movements, NATO maneuvers and suchlike."

They were in a tavern on the wharf. It was the first time in many missions, but since he was supposed to be enjoying a well-earned R and R, the soldier had decided to sink a few beers. The man in the watch cap, perched on the next bar stool, had started talking as soon as he sat down.

"How come they dock in your town?" Bolan asked.

"There's a NATO goodwill flotilla heading this way—frigates from Britain, the U.S., West Germany and Norway—and like I say, they aim to keep tabs. Times they refuel, too, or take shelter from the big storms. It can get kind of rugged out there." The sailor nodded toward the shower of arctic spray exploding over the seawall outside the windowpanes.

"They got a right to put in anyway," he added, "We buy our oil from the Soviets. And they started in on a mining concession over by Husavik, in the northeast, a few months past.''

"Oh, yeah? Mining what?" Bolan wasn't really interested but it cost nothing to be polite.

"Search me." The Icelander shrugged. "Minerals. Whatever. They got some crazy rock formations out there. It seems the Russians are flying in plenty of heavy equipment through the airstrip at Husavik."

Bolan signaled the bartender and bought his companion a beer.

"Skoal!" The guy raised his glass and drank. He shook his head. "Crazy world, too, ain't it? Your Navy people use the Keflavik base to monitor the movement of Soviet warships and subs toward the North Atlantic; the Reds use their boats to monitor the movements of your fleet . . . meantime the seabed is a garbage dump of nuclear waste and listening devices."

"Listening devices?"

"Sure." The seaman laughed. "You know what? Last week one of our coast-guard patrol vessels fished up what looked like a rusted mine that had been floating in the water since World War I." He paused for effect. "It was packed with electronic gadgetry so delicate you could have heard the skipper of a nuclear killer sub shaving!"

Bolan laughed dutifully. The conversation was beginning to tire him. He was on vacation, dammit. In any case he had heard it all before.

He finished his beer, told the sailor in the watch cap goodbye and left. It was a long, tortuous drive to Egilsstadir—a hundred miles in a straight line, almost twice that following Iceland's primitive, twisting roads—and he wanted to make it before the light started to fade.

Egilsstadir was located in a long valley brimming with one of the very few forests in the country. The birch and aspen plantations were no more than twelve feet high, but they grew thickly and they were easy on the eye after grueling hours spent circumnavigating the interminable indented fjords gashing the bleak and treeless coastline.

At one point the road crossed the Jokulsa a Fjollum, the river he was to follow in his kayak, on a high, arched bridge of prestressed concrete. Surmounting a bluff some way downstream, he could see hoists and gantries in the center of a camp that housed, he supposed, the engineers exploiting the Russian mining concession.

The airport at Egilsstadir was a single asphalt runway and a small terminal shack. It was also something like a theater restricted to two shows daily—one for the morning Icelandair flight from Reykjavik and one for the afternoon. In between, the apron was deserted, the terminal as silent as the surrounding forest. Two guards, changing shift every four hours, patrolled the perimeter and guarded a freight shed where Bolan's gear should by now be stored.

The car-rental office was closed when he hit town. He left the Mercedes in the yard with money for the repair of the windshield in an envelope tucked beneath a wiper blade. By the time they made a connection between the engineer who had hired a Colt Shogun in Reykjavik and the crazy explorer who had checked in a G-Wagen that didn't belong to him, he would be long gone.

Hefting his two suitcases, Bolan strode along the empty street in the half light. There had been no further signs of pursuit since the firefight by the swamp. There had been no survivors, either. So by now, he hoped, his anonymous enemies would definitely have lost track of their quarry, allowing him to progress, his own innocent plans unimpeded. Dismissing the problem from his mind, he found a modest hotel overlooking the central square and checked in for the night.

RELATIVELY, THE FIELD WAS A HIVE of activity when he arrived to claim his gear the following morning...the Icelandair flight was expected; a private, six-passenger Beechcraft Bonanza was being refueled at the avgas pump; the pilot of a small overhead-wing Cessna 150 was tying down his aircraft at the far end of the ramp. And above the terminal, an executive jet with Russian markings, which had just taken off, circled the field before it flew away toward the east. By the open doors of the freight shed, a forklift truck maneuvered crates of machinery onto a flatbed semi.

Bolan supervised the unloading of his own crates. The ultralight, powered by a 250 cc two-stroke engine positioned between the spars supporting the delta wing, was equipped with skis as well as landing wheels.

Bolan's kayak—a Norwegian polymer version of the American Precision Mirage model, with a low deck and rounded gunwales—was slung between the struts of the undercarriage.

High-energy iron rations, a goose-down sleeping bag, a ground pad, a wet suit, helmet and underwater boots were stowed in PVC sacks inside the kayak's fore and aft compartments along with the two paddles the warrior had chosen. The entire rig took less than half an hour to assemble.

After he had arranged for the ULM to be collected by helicopter from the sinkhole where he intended to drop beneath the ice to the source of the underground river, the Executioner took his place in the open bucket seat of the ultralight and requested permission for takeoff.

The flight had to be approved by the Icelandic coastguard service, and the official okay had come on condition that Bolan was equipped with two-way radio on which he could call for help in case of any accidents. Judging by the expression on the faces of the mechanics and laborers and customs officers gathered on the apron, local opinion seemed convinced that he would need to use it.

The tiny engine sputtered to life. The polished spruce air-screw behind Bolan's seat spun, and the aircraft trundled out to the runway to await takeoff. A green light glowed from the control room above the terminal, and Bolan was on his way.

He had a flight of approximately seventy miles in front of him. For fifty of these he flew southwest, following the up-stream course of the Jokulsa Fljotsdal river until it emerged from a terminal glacier on the fringe of the ice cap. Then he turned through twenty-two and a half degrees and vectored due west for the glacial region known as the Dyng Jujokull, where the sinkhole was located.

For the first few miles the ULM skimmed the surface of a lake, where the river had drowned a long, twisting valley. Then the land rose abruptly to a highland plateau bare of vegetation, an ancient volcanic wilderness that reminded Bolan in its empty desolation of a black Sahara.

So long as he was overflying the river valley, the Executioner kept the ultralight as low as he dared; even at one thousand feet the cold struck like a knife through the ka-pok-lined alpine survival suit and life belt that he wore. But when the barren rock bulk of the six-thousand-foot peak called Snafell materialized beneath a blanket of low cloud to his right, he hauled back the stick and sent the frail machine climbing high. There was no telling what hazardous combination of cold drafts and air pockets he could en-counter above this icy terrain.

Lacking an oxygen mask, Bolan was becoming light-headed when at last he saw, in the distance, the pale im-mensity of the frozen continent that was his target.

The Vatnajokull, eighty-three miles across and fifty from north to south, is an ice cap rather than a single glacier. The surface, unexpectedly, is not blinding white but varies from gray through browns to a slate mauve. Black lakes circle the southern margin and here, fissured away from the ice cliffs at the glacier's edge, float enormous bergs colored king-fisher blue and jade green in the cold northern light.

It took Bolan some time to locate the sinkhole. It was only when he flew to the terminal moraine from which the river he was to follow emerged and then banked through 180 degrees to track back toward the center of the ice mass, that he identified the dark opening in the frozen surface five hundred feet below.

The landing was rough. Jagged furrows crisscrossed the packed ice in all directions. The ultralight bounced once, twice and then, as the starboard ski snapped under a third impact, slewed sideways and slid for fifty yards, jolting the breath from the Executioner's body and bending one of the aluminum spars that acted as an engine support. Luckily the kayak was undamaged.

Bolan climbed down and began to dismantle the ULM. The sky was darkening ominously and he feared one of Iceland's sudden storms was brewing.

He was not mistaken. Within minutes angry clouds boiled overhead; the wind, penetratingly cold to start with, had howled up to gale force; and squalls of freezing snow lashed horizontally across the surface of the ice.

Bolan was forced to wait out the blinding blizzard. With wind and cold combining to produce a chill factor of minus-thirty-five degrees Fahrenheit, he rigged a hasty shelter from two paddles, the ultralight's unbroken ski and the red and yellow nylon of the machine's delta wing.

After an hour of frozen hell the wind dropped and the sky cleared. Shivering, Bolan emerged from his makeshift tent, unzippered one of his supply sacks and changed into his caver's rig. Beneath the life jacket he wore cellular inners, a Transat neoprene wet suit and a proofed coverall with built-in knee pads to minimize bruising against the inside of the canoe when shooting rapids.

Apart from the helmet, the total effect was much as though he had donned his familiar blacksuit.

Eleven inches of snow had fallen during the storm. Bolan slid the kayak over to the edge of the sinkhole and busied himself with ice clamps, pitons and the arrangement of rope and pulleys that would allow him single-handed to lower himself and his craft into the depths.

The rig was in place before he heard the airplane.

Subconsciously he had for some time been aware of the approaching drone, but it was not until the pilot made his first pass over the cleft that Bolan registered the fact that he was under surveillance from above. It was a small aircraft of a type unfamiliar to him—a V-tail, low-wing monoplane with a single motor in the nose. As it banked and turned for a second run, he could see through the spinning disk of the airscrew that there were two helmeted figures behind the Plexiglas canopy.

A coast-guard patrol, confirming that he had survived the long flight in the ULM? A meteorology crew checking out the results of the storm, astonished to see a human being in this wilderness? Or a private flyer from one of the many small fields that dotted the barren countryside?

It was only when the plane made its third pass—skimming no more than twenty feet above the snow-covered ice—that Bolan realized it carried no markings at all.

Half-deafened by the roar of the engine as it zoomed directly overhead, he watched the machine climb steeply and fly away toward the northeast.

What the hell?

The machine was as anonymous as the hardmen he had wasted in Reykjavik and elsewhere. Bolan tried to make a connection. Had the mystery pursuers latched on to him one more time? If they had, what would their next move be? Bolan shrugged away the questions. The answers could wait. Right now he had more important things to do.

The sinkhole was like a huge inverted tunnel, 70 feet across at the top and more than 150 deep.

A freshening wind and freezing temperatures made the manipulation of ropes and tackle difficult for chilled hands topside. But within the shaft, which had been formed by steam from geothermal vents, the air was warm.

Testing his anchorages one final time, Bolan lowered away the loaded kayak and then swung himself over the edge of the yawning chasm.

At once he was in a different world.

Weathered as an ancient rock face, the walls of the shaft were circled in different layers, each, like the rings in a tree, witness to a different era in the ice cap's twenty-thousand-year history.

The Executioner had to reposition ice screws and take extra turns on the rope as the up current of warm air loosened and then started to melt the surface. It was easier going down than up, but without the crampons clamped to his boots and the pitons he hammered in afresh every ten feet or so, it would have been a rugged—maybe damaging—descent.

He was halfway down, and the light from the opening far above was fast fading, before the whine of wind passing the sinkhole was drowned by the suck and gurgle of water from below. At the same time he became aware that it was uncomfortably hot beneath the protective clothing he wore.

Bolan had made perhaps 120 feet when the ice walls slanted away into the darkness on all sides and he was left dangling in space, suspended above a giant cavern beneath the glacier.

Now the roar of underground waters was loud in his ears. Cautiously, hand over hand, he lowered himself to the last knotted length of rope until his feet submerged and then grounded on solid rock.

Warm water gushed around his knees. A strong current knocked pebbles against his ankles.

Bolan waded across to a shelf, where the hollowed ice wall rested on glistening bedrock. He unbolted the shackles and released the kayak from its rope, stowing the craft safely on the ledge out of reach of the frothing torrent.

Unpacking a powerful flashlight, he flicked it on, then swung right and left to examine the base from which his perilous journey would start.

The cavern was huge. The beam was not strong enough to illuminate its inner recesses. Channeled between smooth islands of rock, the underground river ran fast and deep toward the mouth of a tunnel. At the far end it would, Bolan knew, burst through the Vatnajokull's terminal moraine and emerge into the open air. He intended to be with it.

Playing the beam from water to rock to ice, he marveled at the paradox of nature that permitted this age-old frozen massif to remain unmelted above active subterranean volcanoes spewing out molten lava and creating enough hot springs to provide half the country with domestic warmth.

Too bad the humans up top whose convictions ran to equally opposite extremes had not yet learned to compromise in the same way and exist together in peace.

Yeah, there was a lesson to be learned here if only animal man would check his downward rush long enough to pause and think.

Mack Bolan laid out the ground pad and sleeping bag on the driest part of the shelf he could find, ate a portion of his iron rations and turned in for the night. The pale disk of sky overhead had already darkened to what passed for night in this sub-Arctic summer, and he had to rely on an early start if he was to cross the underground section of his route and make good time through the headwaters of the Jokulsa a Fjollum tomorrow.

FOUR HOURS LATER he was lowering the kayak into the stream. Settled in the cockpit, he adjusted the black neoprene spray skirt around his waist and tightened the elastic draw-cord that fixed it in a watertight seal around the cockpit coaming.

The light filtering down from the sinkhole that was now his sole link with the outside world had already brightened. Bolan clipped the flashlight into its special harness, switched on, fisted his two-blade laminated hardwood paddle and headed with swift, precise strokes for the tunnel mouth.

The first ten minutes of the journey, before he had become accustomed to the speed of the river and the darkness outside of the flashlight beam, were hair-raising.

At first the channel remained smooth and deep, the water speeding almost soundlessly, the boater required only to dip an occasional blade in a brace that would push the kayak away from either of the rock walls rushing past. Then the stream divided around a massive rock, divided again, and there was white water on every side.

The flashlight beam careened wildly out of line as the lightweight craft scythed through tows of two-foot high waves. Water washed over the deck and pummeled the spray skirt. Black fingers of rock reached threateningly through the foaming tide.

Bolan leaned expertly into the swirls of current, his paddle flashing left and right, forcing the kayak into the main channel that had been gouged by the racing river.

Beyond the rapid, the stream was wider and shallower. And now the spray-loaded darkness was loud once more with the sound of rushing water. The vessel swept around a wide curve in the subterranean torrent, and Bolan was drenched in an icy cascade when the kayak shot through a shaft of freezing water thundering down from an opening in the glacier overhead.

Here near the river's source, the boiling flow from geothermal springs mixed with such icy spills to produce an average temperature of ninety-five degrees—a little below blood heat. The layer of moisture inside Bolan's wet suit, acting as an insulator against eventual cold, had been raised the few degrees necessary to make up the difference. But the unexpected freezing spray penetrating the neoprene seals of the suit made the warrior temporarily catch his breath.

It was the subsequent warm flow of blood on super-cooled skin—plus a stinging sensation in the lobe of his left ear and the realization that the chin strap of his helmet had snapped—that alerted him to the danger even before the sound of the shot echoed thunderously around the ice cavern.

5

Bolan's reactions were precise and immediate. He killed the light and stowed the paddle. Then he leaned inward, letting the kayak drift with the swift current, coaxing it toward a rock overhang bordering the outer margin of the river bend.

He felt the lightweight hull nudge the rock. The stern swung around, leaving the bow facing upstream in the dark.

Bolan reached above his head, feeling for a projection that might break the smooth curve of rock. The kayak's gunwale was scraping the water-sculptured rock surface. It could be heard over the ripple and bubble of the stream.

His fingers lodged in a crevice... held on, steadying the craft against the pull of the current.

There had been no second shot. No muzzle-flash had showed against the myriad reflections glinting from wet rock and water and the ice roofing the cavern. But Bolan figured the sniper must be on the far side of the bend in the river since that position would give a marksman the best view— and the longest time to take aim at a target being swept downstream. Now he would be holding his fire, awaiting some give-away move on the part of the target.

In total darkness the Executioner held his breath, straining every sense to locate the invisible killer's fire point. With his free hand, Bolan released one side of the spray skirt from the coaming and groped stealthily inside for the waterproof satchel holding his two guns.

Right now the number-one priority was survival.

The AutoMag possessed greater stopping power, but in these conditions, with distances and deflections as yet unknown, the Beretta's longer range and marginally greater accuracy outweighed Big Thunder's skull-busting impact. Thumbing open the clasps of the satchel, Bolan withdrew the Italian death bringer and eased off the safety.

He couldn't believe that the tiny click was audible over the roaring rush of water, but a blinding light blazed instantly to life, swung across the turbulent current and homed in on the kayak. The beam, more powerful than his own, had lanced out—as he had guessed—from the far side of the bend, exposing him against the rock in the light's pitiless glare.

The warrior could deal with one or more snipers, but not spotlit as vulnerably as an insect pinned to a board. He triggered off a 3-shot burst that smashed the light. At the same time he relaxed his grip on the rock and shoved the kayak violently out into midstream.

The assassin fired again, a hail of lead that chiseled splinters from the rock and stung Bolan's face as the craft spun once, twice, and then whirled away into the blackness.

Bolan knew now—he was facing an assault rifle, fashioned for single shot or full-auto use.

He allowed the kayak to ground on the inside of the bend, downstream from the gunner now but still on the opposite bank. Snapping off the spray skirt, he wedged the boat between two boulders and heaved himself out of the cockpit.

He was waist deep in warm water, the 93-R held high.

His most vital objective was to keep the kayak—and his own lamp—undamaged. Entombed beneath three thousand feet of solid ice, with God knew how many divergent channels and cataracts in the darkness ahead and no hope of finding the sinkhole and climbing out, he would be lost if the boat was punctured or there was no light to guide him.

He waded out toward the center of the flow.

Froth forming around his hips was visible. Or maybe some small unexpected noise, some subtle change in the myriad level of sound tipped the ambusher off.

Hellfire ripped out from the rocky bank.

A deadly hail splatted into the water as Bolan lifted his feet and thrust himself farther downstream.

But his gun hand was well above the surface... and this time there were muzzle-flashes to aim at.

Before the long burst of automatic fire was exhausted he touched down on the riverbed, steadied himself against the tug of the water and loosed off three triple bursts.

Livid flame flickered in turn from the Beretta, momentarily printing the image of the cavern against the dark as the rock walls hurled back the reports in shattering confusion, explosion drowning echo until the reverberations faded into the distance.

The 9 mm death bringers found their mark. Bolan heard a strangled cry followed by a loud splash. A moment later the stream swept something heavy and inert against his legs and then carried it away.

He moved cautiously to the far bank. The killer might not have been alone.

He wasn't.

Bolan heard a voice raised in query. He could even distinguish a slither of feet over the sounds of the river. A faint glimmer of a flashlight, a hand-held model, far less powerful than the one Bolan had destroyed, wavered someplace above the rock shelf, where the marksman had been located. The question was repeated.

Either the backup man must have been deafened by the sounds of the river, or he hadn't realized how far the engagement had gone. There were four rounds left in the Beretta's magazine. Bolan set two of them free.

The 93-R bucked in his hand, choking out its lethal message. The walls of the cavern repeated it. The torchlight beam described an arc over the edge of the shelf and plummeted down toward the water, carrying its owner with it.

For an instant the illumination reappeared beneath the hurrying flow. Then, lit from beneath, the surface froth turned pink, darkened to scarlet, clouded over and finally raced away into the blackness.

There was no more movement from the ledge above the water.

Bolan pulled himself out from the river, retrieved his own heavy flashlight and climbed to the ledge. Empty cans of Icelandic beer, cigarette butts and husks of cheese, bread and fruit showed that the would-be murderers had been there some time. But the eye-opener for the Executioner was the surface of the shelf itself.

The spent shells glistening in the beam of his flashlight lay scattered on a level concrete platform that led back to an alcove hollowed from the cavern wall in which were stowed cartons of food and drink, an inflatable rubber raft and a sophisticated radio transceiver that sat on a wooden bench.

The killers had been lying in wait for him all right. But this was no hasty ambush set up following a report from the airplane that had overflown the ULM while Bolan was preparing his descent into the sinkhole.

What he was looking at was a lookout post that had clearly been in existence for some time.

Bolan switched off the light and sat down in the dark. The questions clamoring for an answer could be put off no longer.

Were these cavern killers, the guys piloting the unidentified airplane and the hardmen making the four previous attempts on his life part of the same team, working out of the same base?

It would be crazy to think otherwise.

Was there something, anything at all that he had noticed that could be a clue to their identity?

Negative.

Clearly, knowing Bolan's reputation and seeing him arrive in Iceland, they had mistakenly assumed he was on the track of some evil project that they were planning. Was there any indication what this could be?

Uh-uh.

Were the lethal methods of "dissuasion" they practiced angled specifically at Mack Bolan, or would they be contingency plans designed to stop *anyone* wising themselves up on the project?

Until now Bolan had assumed they were specific, but the ambush proved otherwise.

He was sitting in what was obviously a permanent lookout post; materials to fashion a concrete platform and install a two-way radio could hardly have been conveyed to a location deep inside the biggest glacier in Europe in a matter of hours or even days. The place had to have been in existence before he even knew himself that he would be boating past it.

The gunmen had been stationed there to block any caver or canoeist who figured he might like to make it along the underground headwaters of the Jokulsa a Fjollum.

Another thought occurred to Bolan—the river must somehow during its course hold the secret these guys were so anxious to keep under wraps.

So what the hell could be so special about a river that rose in an inaccessible subterranean cave and then ran more than one hundred miles through some of the world's coldest, bleakest country?

He had to find out. Because one thing was now crystal clear.

Whatever he may have thought after the earlier attacks, the Executioner's own standpoint was now radically changed.

He decided to carry on with his planned itinerary; there was nothing else he could do. But the aim of the operation would be different. As of now.

To hell with the R and R. This was no longer a vacation trip. No way. The kayak voyage was now a fact-finding mission. Yeah, the unknowns had tried Mack Bolan's patience too far.

He would find out what was brewing along the course of the damned river and put a stop to it.

Or die in the attempt.

Bolan smiled grimly. It seemed he was back on a search-and-destroy kick after all. Despite all those innocent holiday plans. Just the way his unknown enemies had figured he was since the takeoff. They had talked him into it!

He rose and stretched. Suddenly aware that blood still dripped from his ear, he realized that he had completely forgotten that first shot, the very near-miss that had almost ended the Bolan legend.

Adrenaline was the answer. The stuff had been raging through his veins faster than the river ran, fast enough to momentarily make him forget that murderous initial attack until the threat had been mastered by the violence it unleashed.

Yet it was no more than an abrupt swirl in the stream, or maybe an unexpected roll of the kayak's hull, that had saved the warrior's life—a deflection of one single inch in the wrong direction and the killer slug would have severed the carotid artery, wasting his lifeblood in less than two minutes. It would have been Bolan's body then that was washed anonymously away to rot in some backwash creek below the ice-cap mountain. A chilling thought.

He eased off the helmet with its dangling strap.

The wound was no more than a scratch, a raw furrow at the tip of the lobe. He found a thin spray of icy water cascading from a cleft in the rock and bathed the wound alternately with this and the warm water from the river until the bleeding stopped.

Some you win...! Bolan said to himself. He smiled again. And froze.

Gutturally, from someplace behind, a deep voice had boomed in reply. And amid a stream of words incomprehensible among the hollow echoes of the cavern, he had caught the three syllables of his own name.

Mack Bolan.

It was a moment before he caught on; the voice came from the speaker of the radio stashed in the rock alcove.

Base called the lookouts to check whether or not the Executioner had showed. Not so strange.

What did jolt Bolan was the fact that the voice was speaking in Russian.

6

Bolan whistled softly. Pieces of the puzzle locked snugly into place. He remembered the Soviet factory ship at Akureyri, the seaman in the watch cap, snatches of conversation.

Stuff that bored him then had now, suddenly, become loaded with significance.

We buy our oil from the Soviets . . . they got a right to put in here . . . they started a mining concession . . . the Russians are flying in heavy equipment through Husavik.

Right.

Husavik was not far from Jokulsa a Fjollum. From a bluff overlooking the river he was now navigating, Bolan had seen the mine workings during his drive from Akureyri to Egilsstadir.

It all fit. He figured the workings were no more than a cover for some illicit activity connected with the river. And the lookout post beneath the glacier—maybe one of several along the river's course—was just a fail-safe precaution to make sure nobody stumbled on the secret.

If that was so, it was no surprise the plotters had gotten nervous when the Executioner showed . . . and announced his intention to explore the Jokulsa a Fjollum!

And that would be reason enough for the chain of attempts by the death squads to write him off. Because they would have to get him out of the way, whether he was making the trip because he knew about the plot or just by coincidence.

And the hardmen he wasted could well have been Russians. Their MO, too—especially the hypo-and-brandy ploy at the Reykjavik hotel—was worthy of the KGB at that insidious organization's most devious.

But if a corner of the puzzle was now completed, the center remained blank.

Bolan knew who his enemies were and why they wanted him fixed. For good. But he was no nearer uncovering the secret they were so anxious to protect.

What could the Russians be planning in *Iceland*? ICBM silos? Antimissile sites?

No way. With the ranges at their disposal firing from home, who needed Iceland?

Launching pads for cruise missiles or short-range nukes aimed, on the Cuban pattern, at NATO shipping or the more vulnerable countries belonging to the alliance?

Uh-uh. No mine workings could serve as a cover for that kind of stuff. Practically every town in the country boasted an airstrip—there would be far too many overflights by coast-guard choppers and private planes for surface projects of that nature to remain undetected. In any case the concession was officially leased; plant was being flown in openly; presumably the authorities enjoyed some kind of inspection facility.

It seemed obvious, too, that the whole deal was tied in with the river. And the sailor in Akureyri had mentioned Red navy specialists.

Some kind of marine detection unit then? Some monitoring aid for those so-called factory ships in the North Atlantic? Something in any case that must, for Bolan's money, be located underground? Or underwater?

Whatever, he would find out the truth.

BOLAN DRANK A CAN OF BEER, helped himself to some fruit that was left in the alcove and returned to the kayak. The

Russian voice on the radio was still querulously demanding news. Bolan switched on the light, pushed himself out into midstream and continued his journey.

The two snipers he had killed had used an inflatable raft to reach their lookout post. Even with rapids and an occasional waterfall, this had to mean that the river, from here on down to its exit from beneath the glacier, was largely navigable.

No class-six stretches of white water, no cascades dropping over unclimbable shelves, no tunnels with roofs too low to allow a canoeist to pass.

Bolan wondered if there would be other, more dangerous obstacles. A second lookout post, for instance, with more alert patrols?

He guessed not. There was no other entry to the subterranean watercourse; one post between the sinkhole and the exit would surely be enough.

That didn't rule out the possibility of an emplacement somewhere along the Vatnajokull's terminal moraine. That was where he would install a backup team himself, if he was determined to block all boating on the upper part of the river.

He guessed right on both counts.

But before he saw the sky again, there were natural hazards to overcome.

The river twisted through caverns no more than ten feet high, ran out across vast chambers whose roofs were lost in darkness far above the flashlight's range. At times it flowed fast and deep, then bubbled over rock steps, where there was scarcely enough draft to float the kayak.

Other times the waterway lost itself in underground lakes so wide it was hard to locate the main channel among the network of passages.

Bolan steered past chutes of freezing water, hot geysers that spewed mud through the surface of the stream, tributary falls that thundered in his ears and veiled the flashlight beam with mist.

He encountered only three major difficulties.

The first was a cataract where the river divided into tiny streams that ran for what seemed hundreds of yards over a slope of smooth pebbles and forced him to carry the kayak on his back while he maneuvered the light to show up treacherous bed beneath the shallow water.

The second could have buried him beneath the Vatnajokull for keeps.

He chose the wrong outlet on the far side of a deep, still lake and found himself being carried faster and faster by a strong current that flowed between narrowing walls and a roof so low that he could barely wield his paddle. Then, as he realized his mistake, the stream careered away at right angles and poured through an arch into a basin hollowed from the rock at a much lower level.

Desperately Bolan flexed his feet against the pegs, straining knees against the control bracings as he dug a blade hard in and leaned against the remorseless pull of the water to bring the kayak broadside onto the flow.

The vessel swung slowly, too slowly, around. The current jammed it fast across the opening. The fiberglass hull creaked as water roared past and down.

Bolan was thankful for the mishap. The water was too deep to stand in; in any case the current would have swept him away through the narrow opening. The pool into which it plunged was at least thirty feet below, judging by the sound of the fall. And even if he survived the drop, he could never get out alive.

Shakily he unfastened the spray skirt and half rose, reaching for the rock above the opening. He figured that if he was strong enough to maneuver the craft away from the arch and force it along the wall, against the current, until it was safe to swing around and use the paddle again, there was a risk the hull might be damaged against the abrasive basalt.

It was a risk he had to take.

Bolan was accustomed to them. And here he had no choice.

He was in good physical shape, but even with his immense strength and determination it was more than thirty minutes before he shoved the kayak out from the wall, grabbed the paddle in his raw, bleeding hands and used his remaining energy in a battle against the current.

The third difficulty was too damned close for comfort.

It happened as the river, wide now and flowing swiftly, rounded a sharp curve.

He was suddenly confronted by a single wave, four feet high and boiling above a rockfall, scouring a line of swirling suckholes from the riverbed beyond. And in the center of the flow, immediately ahead of the canoe, stood a jagged column that must have fallen from the roof too recently for water to have planed away the cruel edges.

If the kayak was dashed against that wicked rock, Bolan knew he could kiss the rest of the trip goodbye.

Maybe the rest of his life, too.

The maneuver was not all that difficult for an experienced canoeist. It was the suddenness of the rock's appearance, whirling out of the dark only feet away from the flashlight, and the lightning speed with which he had to take evasive action that taxed Mack Bolan's honed reactions to their limits.

He plunged the paddle deep into the water, then shifted his weight and slalomed the kayak through 180 degrees to face upstream.

Then a single savage bite with the square-tipped blade thrust them aside into the primary channel.

After that there was no time for anything but prayer.

Sucked onward by the accelerating flood, the kayak surfed the wave stern first, barely missing the deadly rock. The craft shuddered crazily, almost capsized in the wild water...and at last floated out into the center of a placid pool three hundred feet wide.

Bolan grasped the paddle and propelled the kayak toward the far side of the pool with swift, sure strokes.

Ten minutes later, the darkness thinned, dissolved, and the lightweight craft glided out between dirty gray ice crags into the open air.

THE SNIPERS WERE POSTED behind a group of boulders a mile downstream from where the river emerged.

There were, in fact, Bolan discovered, several streams flowing out from beneath the glacier. Some meandered through the conglomerate of rocks, stones, mud and sand scoured from the earth's surface by the glacier and deposited around its outer fringe. Some formed pools in which ice masses, broken off from the main flow, floated like miniature bergs. Some channeled straight through the moraine to join the main stream.

A dozen hit teams would have been needed to cover all these exits. It was logical therefore, the Executioner reasoned, that the Russians would wait until all these watercourses joined to form one waterway and place a single patrol there.

But the theory had to be checked. He beached the kayak on a gravel spit where the last tributary flowed in and climbed a fifteen-foot bank of shale to make his initial recon.

It was late afternoon. Low cloud cover transformed the sky into a uniform gray. A chill wind blew over a bare rock plateau that stretched as far as he could see in every direction.

Crouched low so that he would not be silhouetted against the skyline, Bolan scanned the bleak terrain. The dun-colored plateau—eroded remains of an age-old lava flow—was marked with a darker, winding trail that charted the course of the river.

A quarter mile away, the channel gouged from the basalt looped into a wide oxbow. It was on the outside of this curve, Bolan guessed, that a backup team would most likely be posted.

He was right.

It was hard to see at first, because a camouflage tarp had been rigged above the emplacement to minimize detection from the air. But there was movement above a rockfall rampart, a dull glint of metal, maybe a reflection from a pair of binoculars, that attracted Bolan's attention.

He guessed there were two gunners beneath the tarp. Perhaps three. And he had to take them out before continuing his voyage, although, with every voice that failed to respond to radio queries from base, the vigilance of the Soviet HQ personnel would be sharpened and increased.

The snipers were alert, too. Discreet as Bolan's movements had been, they were spotted by the lookouts. He saw rock chips fly and heard the screech of a ricochet before the crisp, sharp explosion of the rifle shot reached him.

The marksman fired twice more before Bolan dropped from sight, momentarily shaken. The gunner was a fair shot, considering the distance.

Bolan felt the hot wind of one slug above his hair; the other sliced a fragment of rock away moments before he was to grab it as a handhold. The soldier decided it was health-ier down by the riverside!

Reinstalled in the kayak, the warrior allowed himself to drift downstream between the rocky banks, using the pad-dle only if the craft threatened to backtrack into an eddy or snag on an obstruction. He left the spray skirt stowed in the bow compartment—the river ran smooth and fairly deep here, and he might have to spring out in a hurry.

He was, he judged, two bends above the oxbow when a sight line past a two-hundred-yard reach and between two opposing bluffs gave him a glimpse of the killers' hideout.

It was a momentary view, before the emplacement disappeared behind one of the bluffs. But it was not reassuring.

One guy was left beneath the tarp, toting what looked like a submachine gun. Two others had left the shelter, one on either side, to scramble away between the boulders. Each had a hunting rifle slung across his back.

But they weren't after caribou, Bolan felt certain. The Russians were planning to bracket him with a double enfilade.

He took up the paddle and pin-wheeled the canoe out into the center of the current. With swift strokes he belted the craft toward the nearer of the two bluffs. A couple of handguns, however efficient and however skilled the shooter, were no match for the weapons arrayed against him. Especially if he was going to be under fire from three separate points.

There was no way he could shoot his way out of this one in open confrontation—stealth and wits were the operative words. And the number-one priority there was to find a hiding place.

He stroked the kayak into a pool hollowed from the basalt and overhung by a shelf of harder rock. Here he would be visible only to someone standing immediately opposite on the other side of the river.

Right now there was no watcher. But Bolan's own view was similarly restricted. He climbed out of the kayak and waded to the inner margin of the pool. He carried the Beretta, its 20-round magazine in place, in his right hand. The

.44 AutoMag, fully loaded, was stashed inside the zippered front of his wet suit.

He trod across a narrow strip of shingle and hauled himself up onto the projecting shelf. The sound of the water cascading from his wet suit would be lost in the burble of the river.

From the shelf there was a wider view of the far bank, of the boulders bordering the entrance to the oxbow, of the bare plateau above.

But there was no sign of the Russians. The emplacement was out of sight around the bend. Nothing moved among the rocks at the edge of the ancient lava flow. No bird flew, no vegetation stirred in the wind, even the lowering clouds appeared stationary.

For Bolan there was only one course of action—he must take out his adversaries one by one. But first he had to know where they were. Before they could become targets for the Executioner's hellfire attacks they had to show themselves.

He decided to draw their fire.

Above the rock shelf, weathered by frost, eroded by millennia of freezing storms, the strata were soft. He broke off a chunk and lobbed it out beyond the ledge to tumble down a shaley slope and splash into the river.

It was the oldest trick in the book.

And it didn't work.

There were no more revealing shots. Nobody plunged down among the boulders to check whether Bolan had missed his footing on the slope. Bolan waited.

There was silence, except for the chuckle of the stream.

The sky darkened, then scattered drops of rain began to fall. Soon the light would thicken into the Icelandic dusk.

Prone on his shelf, the warrior breathed shallowly, every nerve alert for the slither of a foot brushing rock, the click of a cocking hammer, the telltale rattle of a stone.

He heard nothing.

Then suddenly there came a bellow, a harsh voice distorted by a bullhorn.

"Bolan! We know you are there! Come out and surrender and no harm will come to you. Our superiors only wish to ask you some questions. Give yourself up and you will be fairly treated as a prisoner."

Bolan smiled grimly. Fair treatment? Oh, sure—with every imaginable kind of torture they could think of.

"Be sensible, Bolan," the amplified voice continued when he made no reply. "If you do not show yourself we shall come in with grenades."

Bolan replied in Russian. "I am waiting—come and get me!"

There was no further communication from the bullhorn.

Soon afterward, he heard the distant drone of the airplane. He had been expecting it. It didn't bother him. The kayak was beneath the overhang, invisible from the air; Bolan's neoprene wet suit was almost the same color as the basalt. Lying facedown he would be indistinguishable from the rocky background.

It was the same light plane that had checked him out above the sinkhole, he saw from the corner of his eye. The pilot made perhaps a dozen passes over the oxbow and the surrounding wilderness. He flew up and down the course of the river.

Evidently he saw nothing and his radio reports to the emplacement were negative, because there was no reaction from the hidden gunmen. Soon the plane vanished in the darkening sky to the north.

The rain fell more heavily, dimpling the surface of the river. Wind moaned through crevices in the lava massifs. Bolan was shivering, the insulating layer of moisture inside his wet suit chilled by inactivity.

When it was dark, he clambered down to the pool, ate and drank, and then made some changes to the loading of the kayak.

He stowed a spare paddle, a two-piece model assembled with an aluminum sleeve and a set screw, in the stern compartment. He snapped the spray skirt in place around the coaming, wedged each of the paddle halves under the belt that normally fit around his waist and then propped them up so that the skirt rose above the level of the deck. He bulked out the tentlike silhouette with PVC sacks from the two storage compartments and laid the one-piece paddle across the foredeck.

Bolan hoped the mock-up could fool watchers into believing here was a boater in the cockpit, hunched up to avoid detection.

Because he had to end this stalemate pretty damned quick—as soon as full daylight returned, he was certain there would be a chopper loaded with reinforcements overhead.

Pushing the kayak in front of him, he waded out into the center of the river. The water reached almost to his armpits; the pull of the current was strong enough to make it hard keeping on his feet.

He shoved the boat away and moved toward the opposite bank, his silenced Beretta held above the surface.

The kayak was carried downstream, gathering speed as the oxbow approached.

Bolan was taking two chances—that the current would dump the canoe in still water at the far end of the oxbow, where he could recover it; secondly that the snipers would fire at what they figured for a man and not the boat, so that damage would be minimal.

The bow of the kayak angled in to the curve.

Bolan heard a shout over the patter of rain on the water. He raised the Beretta, finger curled around the trigger, left hand grasping the foregrip.

Pinpoints of flame flickered high among the boulders. Three single shots came in quick succession. The rifleman was hiding above, behind the shelf on the same side of the river as the overhang.

Had been hiding.

Bolan triggered two bursts before the echoes of the first shot died away, aiming below and fractionally to the left of the rifle's muzzle-flash. The 9 mm skull busters smashed through the killer's rib cage and fisted his life away while two of his own slugs were puncturing the kayak's spray skirt. His third shot went into the sky as he was flung back lifeless among the rocks.

Bolan lifted his feet and allowed the buoyancy of his life jacket to carry him after the kayak.

He approached the curve fifty yards behind the canoe.

Fire spit down on the craft from the bluff on the outer edge of the oxbow. And this time the hardman had allowed the long hours of waiting to sap his concentration. He was silhouetted against the almost dark sky.

Bolan drifted against a rock that showed above the surface of the water. His feet touched ground. He hauled himself out of the river and sighted the 93-R.

The guy was reloading. He had only a 3-shot rifle. Probably a Husqvarna .358 Express. Very long range. Dead accurate. Hyperhigh muzzle velocity that gave the 150-grain slugs an almost flat trajectory and huge knockdown power.

Providing you hit something.

Bolan mowed him down. But not before the gunman had made his play. The executioner must have stirred foam from the surface as he landed. Two shots splatted into the water in front of him; a third caromed off the rock into the night.

By this time the rifleman was on his way. A stream of death had hosed across his chest. The gun splashed into the river; the shooter landed on his back across a narrow crescent of shingle that the current had deposited on the inside of the bend.

Bolan submerged again and swam over there. The guy was dead, open eyes dulled in the northern twilight, his torso black with blood. Two plastic grenades were slipped to his web belt. Bolan unfastened one and went back into the water.

He swam now, openly, a fast crawl that churned the water, and accelerated by the current, brought him rapidly to the apex of the oxbow. The Beretta, together with Big Thunder and the grenade, was belted to his waist in a waterproof sack.

His kayak had been carried around the bend and was now within range of the last Russian beneath the tarp. The guy opened up with his SMG—short, sharp bursts that ripped out with shattering force and stitched the gloom with points of flame.

The kayak appeared to shudder from the force of the shells. It spun, heeled over, righted itself and headed stern first for the opposite bank.

Bolan was below the emplacement, waist high in the stream, the PVC sack unzipped. His right hand dipped in, came out holding the grenade. He pulled the pin. His arm swung back.

As the gunner got wise to the fact that the kayak was pilotless—either that or he had two enemies to deal with!—Bolan uncoiled and pitched.

The grenade streaked through the air, hit the stony rampart and bounced in under the tarp.

The Russian had time to unleash one brief burst in the Executioner's direction before the explosion. The slugs perforated the PVC sack.

Then came the cracking detonation and a livid sheet of yellow flame. Brown smoke laced with scarlet ballooned out and drifted away. The collapsed tarp flared momentarily and then subsided onto the debris of charred flesh and splintered the wooden flooring of the emplacement.

Bolan sighed and headed for the canoe. He would have wished it some other way. But so long as animal man chose to play by the devil's rules...hell, there just *was* no other way.

Grimsstadir, the only village anywhere near the river on the first half of its journey to the sea, was fifty miles downstream. There was an airstrip there and a road junction at the head of a lake. For most of the distance the Jokulsa a Fjollum channeled its course through the bare lava uplands. There was only one other sector where a mountain track veered within half a mile of the river valley.

The Executioner wondered how many more humans he would be forced to kill, how many lookout posts he would have to overcome, before he unearthed the secret of this wild countryside and its clandestine invaders.

7

The kayak was beached, as Mack Bolan had guessed, on the far side of the oxbow.

It was tipped onto its side, with water washing over the coaming and into the cockpit. The spray skirt was riddled with bullet holes, one of the spare paddle halves was snapped in two and several waterproof sacks had been damaged. The fiberglass hull was perforated in twelve places—three individual holes in the foredeck and seven stitched in a near row that slanted from gunwale to keel line.

Bolan removed the contents, inverted the vessel to tip out the water and carried it to a slope of dry rock above the river.

There was a can of resin filler among his supplies, originally included in case the craft was punctured while running the rapids. Working with the help of the flashlight beam, he plugged the holes and smoothed over the filler with a palette knife. The repairs might not withstand a battering by submerged rocks in a really rugged stretch of white water, but at least they would keep him afloat.

If he did lose the kayak, he would still follow the river by other means—a rented all-terrain vehicle, on horseback or even on foot. But he was determined to carry out his initial vacation plan. But the overriding priority now was to learn what these Russians were up to. He hoped for their sake that it was not something sinister.

Navymen, commercial personnel or KGB, it was all the same to him—he was personally involved now.

That challenge was enough for the warrior.

He would unravel the mystery, uncover the intruders' plan and wreck the project, whatever it was. Nothing less would satisfy him now.

He would follow the damned thing through to its conclusion, whatever the odds.

And if he drew the short straw, if in the final reckoning those odds ran against him, well, at least he would have tried. The Executioner knew no other way.

As soon as the resin had hardened, Bolan unloaded a spare spray skirt from the storage compartment, relaunched the kayak and sped downriver.

There was obviously a limit to the amount of harassment the Russians could get away with. It was unlikely they would dare operate a full-scale manhunt in a foreign country; even in a remote area such as this there would be the risk of an international incident, repercussions at the United Nations, a threatened breakdown of diplomatic relations.

Helicopter recon flights could be similarly restricted. In a country with an unusual number of small airstrips and many private aircraft flying the domestic airlanes because of the rudimentary surface communications, they would soon be spotted. Such sorties would be counterproductive, drawing attention to a situation the Russians wished to keep secret.

Still, Bolan decided to rest during the hours of full daylight and ride the river only during the short northern half night. He had perhaps two hours left before sunrise. Each precious moment must be used to distance him as far as possible from the destroyed emplacement.

For several miles below the oxbow, the current ran smooth between fifty-foot cliffs channeled from the ancient lava. Then the canyon widened, the margins of the stream drew apart, the landscape flattened even farther into a region of tundra floored with multicolored mosses and patches of lichen covering the rocky outcrops.

Bolan paddled as fast as he could. Beyond the plain, his maps showed another track of volcanic country criss-crossed by steep-sided ravines. And until he reached that, there wasn't a hope in hell of concealment—scarcely a boulder impeded the shallow course of the river as it flowed easily over the flat land, and there was certainly no place a kayak could be hidden.

Bolan's arms moved back and forth with the regularity of a metronome, water droplets trailing from the long paddle, blades biting deep into the current as he forced the craft downstream.

Conical peaks flanked by a line of low hills materialized out of the gloom ahead, but they were still several miles away when the sky lightened in the east and clouds took shape out of the darkness overhead. The rain had stopped but an icy wind still whined across the plain, riffling the surface of the water and scouring the lone boater's face.

Bolan plowed doggedly on. There was nothing else he could do; he had no place else to go.

There were no signs of pursuit by the time, almost an hour later, he stroked the kayak in among the first of the hills. But before he could think of resting there was another major obstacle—the Jokulsa a Fjollum itself.

The river was turning sour on him, and there was fast water ahead!

Huge granite boulders, dumped by some forgotten gla-cier aeons ago, lay strewed across the watercourse, some with their craggy summits above the flow, others sub-merged dangerously close to the surface.

Foaming white water seized the kayak and accelerated it into a cleft between two of these towering sentinels. On the far side Bolan was faced by a ferocious row of high waves, tall whitecaps facing upstream that came pounding down on the bow of his lightweight craft as he sliced a path through the rapid.

The swiftest flow ran along the base of a cliff that rose sheer on his right. He slipped cross-channel, braced momentarily upstream to allow the kayak to be swept into it, then hurtled onward, washed over from bow to stern, his eyes blinded by spray.

A sawtooth rock ridge cut the surface. He braced again to shoot around that, slalomed past a shark fin of basalt and then snapped his hips sideways and paddled fiercely to steer into calmer water as he felt the canoe begin to dump.

It was then that he saw the concrete pumping station built out on a ledge overlooking a river.

And a guy with the machine pistol covering him while the raging current threw them closer together.

Bolan had no choice to lift the spray skirt and reach for one of his own guns—he was too busy using the paddle to keep himself afloat. The guard was on a catwalk surrounding the concrete cabin. When the kayak was within twenty yards, he jerked the muzzle of the machine pistol in an unmistakable order—stroke the kayak into dead water beneath the ledge.

Bolan accepted the invitation.

"You better had come up here," the gunman called in heavily accented English. "It is drier, and you can hide your boat beneath."

The pumping station stood on a platform that projected beyond the ledge, two and a half feet above the surface of the river. Its outer edge was supported on two pillars rising from the water. Bolan unfastened his spray skirt, climbed out of the kayak and slid it in below this makeshift boathouse. He scrambled up a rocky bank and approached the guy with the gun.

It was an Ingram MAC-11, a deadly machine pistol.

The finger on the trigger belonged to a husky dude, almost Bolan's height, with straight blond hair above blue eyes deep set in a tanned weather-beaten face. He was wearing a fisherman's sweater, denim pants and rubber wading boots. He didn't look much like the other hardmen who had tried, unsuccessfully, to get the drop on the Executioner.

But he looked as dangerous.

Bolan halted two feet away at the far end of the catwalk, keeping his hands in sight and well clear of his body. He eyed the flesh-shredder held unwaveringly in the guy's big hands.

"Who are you? What do you want?" he asked evenly—realizing as he heard the sound of his own voice that these were the first words he had spoken in his own language since he left Egilsstadir almost forty-eight hours before.

"I wish only to talk," said the man holding the Ingram. "You and me, I think we maybe are fighting on the same side."

8

His name was Gunnar Bjornstrom. He was an Icelandic citizen, Bolan learned, but his family came from Norway. Before that, there was a brief interrogation.

"You are Mack Bolan, the man known as the Executioner?"

Bolan did not deny it.

"More recently known as Colonel John Phoenix, of Stony Man Farm, in Virginia?"

"Recently? It seems a long time ago," Bolan said.

"You have waged what they call a one-man war against, first, the Mafia, and then terrorists all over the world?"

"What of it?"

"And lately it is against the KGB especially that you have been fighting?"

"You are well informed."

"It is important that I know who you are," the Icelander said.

"Look, you've got the drop on me with that." The soldier nodded toward the SMG. "So what do you intend to do?" Even as he spoke the warrior sensed that this man was not the enemy.

"So what do you do in Iceland, Mr. Bolan?" Bjornstrom asked in turn, ignoring Bolan's question.

"I'm on vacation," Bolan said.

"A vacation? And you shoot always on vacation some Russians maybe? In caverns and along the river at night? You are on a hunting trip perhaps—hunting for men?"

"I planned to make a source-to-mouth trip along this river. Some guys tried to kill me for no apparent reason. So I killed them."

Bjornstrom smiled. Strong teeth flashed white against the tan of his face. "I am coming upriver myself when you fight. So I halt myself to see what happen."

"Thanks for your help!" Bolan said dryly.

"You do not understand. First, I have to know where you fight. I mean on which side."

"So it *is* a fight, is it?"

Bjornstrom shrugged. "A fight. An investigation. A curiosity to satisfy. Call it what you want."

"Okay, so who are you working for?"

"I am very inquisitive man," Bjornstrom said evasively. "When I see strangers making much secret work in my country—strangers who pretend they operate only a mining concession—I ask myself why. I ask myself why they wish nobody along the river, why they have gunmen beneath Vatnajokull when the concession is more than one hundred miles away. I ask myself but there is no answer. So I try to find out myself."

"You won't believe this, but I am asking myself exactly the same questions," Bolan said.

"But you, too, no answers?"

"Not yet, my friend. But I will get answers."

Bjornstrom lowered the Ingram and held out his hand. "Is good. Is very good. Maybe we better can work together then?"

"Suits me," Bolan said, taking the man's powerful grasp. The soldier remained skeptical about the story of a private citizen's fact-finding crusade. But the truth could wait—instinctively he trusted this big man, and the Executioner always backed his own hunches. "But I have to tell you," he added, "I found out nothing so far. You do any better, working upstream?"

"A little." Bjornstrom shrugged again. "They are using the hot water from beneath the ice; they tap the supply in their own pipes and again from the installation here."

"Here?" Bolan stared at the pump house. It was about twice the size of a beach cabin, a flat-roofed, windowless rectangle with a louvered metal door secured by a padlock and chain. From inside, he could hear a mechanical whine over the roar of tumbling water. "How come?" he asked.

"I show you." Bjornstrom led the way around the catwalk to the rear of the building. Three pipes emerged from a rocky bank to pierce the wall below the catwalk. Two of them were large-bore aluminum-based tubes eighteen inches in diameter; the third, half hidden beneath them, was much smaller.

"That one, the plastic, the Russians have placed." Bjornstrom indicated the smaller pipe. "She stays with the others all the way to the booster station at Grimsstadir. Then they take her in a different direction, toward the estuary."

"You're saying they secretly laid down...?" Bolan shook his head. "I don't get it. Surely this installation is government property."

Bjornstrom nodded.

"Well, don't they check it out? Don't they make inspections from time to time? I mean won't someone get wise to that third pipe?"

"There is nothing to check," the Icelander said. "The turbines are water driven. The pipe does not show from the air. Maybe once in two years someone comes past; but maybe that man is paid by the Russians not to see that third pipe. Unless a fault operates some warning light at the center there is no reason for an inspection."

Bolan looked dubious. "You mean they pipe *hot* water all that way? Over one hundred miles? That's crazy. I mean the heat loss . . ." He shook his head again.

"The Icelanders are ingenious," Bjornstrom said, smiling. "There are many volcanoes beneath the ground, not just at Vatnajokull; many geysers, many hot springs. All the time they are adding more. To keep up the temperature, for the towns and villages. You know?"

"Why would the Russians need it?"

"Like us, to keep warm maybe. To save putting in expensive plant, to save oil. We are almost at Arctic Circle. It is very cold where they work below sea."

"Below *sea*?"

"But yes. Well, below the water in the fjord anyway."

"They have underwater workings on that mining concession?"

"Yes. But I do not think it is just for mining."

"Right," Bolan said. "I figure the mining routine strictly for a front. But a front for what?"

"This is what I wish to find out."

"You got any ideas?"

"Not so far. From the water there is only cliffs to see, and it is not possible to get inside the concession—they have guards and a wire fence. Also only Russians work there; there are no local laborers employed. In any case, I think the real work will not be showing above ground."

"I guess not. Everything on this deal centers around water—the glacier, the river, this goddamn pipe. And now you say the workings are below sea level, too. What the hell can they be doing?"

Bjornstrom was about to reply when suddenly he held up a hand in warning. In the distance, over the roar of water they could hear the rotor whine of a jet helicopter. "I think maybe it would be good if we are hiding just now," he said.

Bolan was moving before Bjornstrom finished speaking.

They vaulted the rail and flattened themselves against the wall beneath the catwalk.

The chopper was flying very low. It was a WSK Swidnik recon helicopter. The sliding panel on the port side of the Plexiglas bubble was locked back. A gunner cradling a SMG stood braced in the opening, scanning the terrain below. Beyond him, they could see the pilot hunched over his controls. Both wore anonymous gray combat fatigues, like the hardcases who had previously tried to eliminate the Executioner.

The engine roar crescendoed and then began to fade as the Swidnik passed overhead, following the course of the river.

"I guess they will fly as far as the outpost you smashed," Bjornstrom said, "and then return, trying to locate the man who did that."

"Could be." Bolan nodded. "They'll certainly be wise to the fact it's a no-go situation up there. The radio's dead. But, like you say, they'll probably check there first."

They were both wrong.

Beneath the catwalk they were hidden from a plane approaching from the north, and invisible when it was overhead. But the platform was not wide enough to hide them from a southern approach—or from anyone heading south who looked back over his shoulder.

The Russian with the subgun looked over his shoulder.

His head ducked back inside the Plexiglas blister. The chopper hung on its blades in a tight U-turn and flew back downstream.

Bolan was already waist deep in water beneath the ledge, groping inside the kayak for his weapons.

Bjornstrom dodged around the corner of the pump house. The helicopter sideslipped to keep him in view, lost height, then hovered to allow the guy with the SMG to line up on the Icelander below.

That was the pilot's mistake.

The gunner sprayed hot lead. Chips of concrete flew from the pump-house wall. The slugs gouged long splinters of wood from the planking above Bjornstrom's head. White water jetted high into the air as one of the pipes was drilled. But Bjornstrom, standing unafraid among the death hail, had already raised the muzzle of his Ingram.

Gritting his teeth, he held the jackhammering machine pistol on full-auto until the 30-round magazine emptied itself.

He did not aim at the Russian, but at the rotors above him, allowing the natural muzzle climb of the gun's incredible 1200 rpm firing rate to rake the entire diameter of the whirling arc.

Encountering a relentless stream of 9 mm parabellums, the effect was as if the rotors had slammed into a solid iron bar. The blades sheared, sending fragments spinning all over the sky. The drive shaft, freed of load, screamed up the scale. The helicopter lurched onto its side and fell.

Spilled from the open cabin, the guy with the gun hurtled out of the aircraft. He landed on a rock in the middle of the rapid, his body split open like a slaughtered animal.

White water whisked his gun away.

On the far bank, the Swidnik hit the ground with a shattering crash, bursting instantly into a blazing fireball as fuel spilled over the hot jet engine.

From the flame-tinged smoke that billowed upward, astonishingly, the figure of the pilot emerged. He was staggering. Blood streamed from a cut above his eye. But the eye itself—malevolently glaring—was fixed steadily on the pump house across the river. And the Tokarev pistol in his hand was aimed directly at Bjornstrom.

With an empty magazine and no refill, the Icelander was helpless, a perfect target against the white wall below the catwalk.

"Dive!" Bolan yelled, thrusting his way through the water, speeding toward the center of the stream.

Bjornstrom flattened himself below the railing as the pilot fired. Copper-jacketed scorchers screamed across the rapid and ricocheted off the platform. In the same movement the Russian swung the Tokarev toward Bolan.

But Big Thunder was already spitting flame. Braced against the stream in a crouched professional stance, the huge cannon bucking in his two-handed grasp, Bolan triggered a series of Magnum exit passes the pilot's way.

The roar of the shots echoed thunderously off the rocky banks. The first of the punishing 240-grain boattails smashed the pistol from the Russian's grip and cored his wrist like a red-hot wire. The second, third and fourth lashed across his chest—steel whips reducing liver, lungs and heart to a bloody pulp in less than a second.

The guy was dead before his gun hit the water. The body, flung backward by the colossal impact of the .44's slugs, punched out at 1640 feet per second, slammed against a granite slope on the riverbank, then slid into the foaming water. It vanished into a suckhole on the far wide of the waves, reappeared bobbing on the surfacc fifty yards downstream and was then swept away.

The wreck of the chopper was still blazing fiercely.

Bolan waded out of the water and rejoined Bjornstrom below the catwalk. "Daylight or no daylight," he said soberly, "we have to get out of here fast." He nodded toward the roiling black column leaning away from the wind above the wreck. "Those guys will have friends...and it won't take an Indian brave to read that smoke signal."

The Icelander nodded in turn. He made no mention of the death they had so narrowly avoided. A strong man, Bolan noted, and one to be relied on in a tight spot.

Still, there were many questions left unanswered. A regular Icelandic civilian who just happened to be satisfying his curiosity? Who happened to own an Ingram? And who happened to be courageous enough to stand up and use it under fire?

But the mystery of Bjornstrom's real identity was a problem that could wait. It was enough for now that he was a friend. A friend in need, at that, Bolan reflected.

"From here," Bjornstrom told him, "we can safely continue even in daylight for maybe twenty miles. After the next bend there is a cascade, and then from high ground to the west a country road overlooks the river. Also there is an airstrip by Herdubreid."

"Say again?"

"The crater of an old volcano. It is at 5500 feet. There may be tourists at this time of year. They could overlook, too. The Russians will not dare attack on that section."

"Uh-huh. The only thing is…" Bolan paused. "Well, the kayak is strictly one-man transport. Especially in this kind of water."

"That is not a problem. I have my own boat."

"That's great. But where—?"

"Below the waterfall. Maybe two hundred yards. It is in a cave, quite hidden."

"You're suggesting we continue in convoy?"

"Yes, if you wish it. I know the river well from a long time. With me you can make it more quickly. When it becomes dangerous again we shall hide and continue by night."

"Sure. That was my plan anyway."

"Then, after Grimsstadir and the lake…we make our own secrets, okay? We disappear until we can make the fjord and discover theirs!"

Bolan punched the Icelander lightly on the shoulder. "We're on our way…."

9

The boat was a powered rubber raft with a 25 hp Excelsior outboard tilted up over the stern. There was more than enough room for two, even with Bolan's supplies and the spare fuel jerricans. But the Executioner preferred to stick with the patched-up kayak—partly because he had no wish to be dependent on Bjornstrom, although the enigmatic Icelander had so far proved a reliable ally, but mainly because he was determined as long as possible to keep up the fiction of his self-imposed vacation task.

Bolan's priority was still to learn the identity of the guys who had decided to eliminate him. But to keep faith with himself was damned near as important. Mack Bolan was not the kind of man who would be content to leave a job unfinished.

There was, too, the matter of logistics. Two crafts would be more difficult for their enemies to destroy than one. Twice as difficult in fact. With two they would have more freedom of movement, and that extra mobility could mean the difference between life and death.

Again, if one was destroyed and the supplies had been equally divided between them, they would not be left with nothing.

It did not even occur to Bolan that both might be destroyed.

As Bjornstrom had said, the twenty miles passed without incident. The river wound its way through narrow defiles, between high banks of volcanic shingle, at the foot of gorges channeled from the rock. They passed black sandbanks, mudflats bubbling with miniature geysers and tributaries of hot water, where the steam blew from the surface like spray on a stormy day.

Herds of wild ponies and an occasional pair of giant crows, riding the wind above the desolate landscape, were the only forms of life they saw until late in the afternoon. Then, far away on a track that climbed a huge mountain slope, they saw the antlike form of some vehicle laboring toward the crest.

Later, hang gliders, a trio of light aircraft and even a solitary ULM passed overhead, all of them presumably from the strip at the foot of the volcanic crater.

Before their ghostly journey through the gloom of the sub-Arctic night they were twice halted by what the tourist guides called "major waterfalls." Bjornstrom proved his worth once more on the first of these, where the widening river slid over a rock shelf to plunge forty feet or more into a foaming pool.

For two miles before the fall, the current flowed smoothly between vertical cliffs of crumbling basalt that towered higher every hundred yards. If the Icelander had not known intimately that reach of the Jokulsa a Fjollum and urged Bolan to disembark the moment the rocky banks closed in, the Executioner would have had to waste precious time backing up, because the eroded lava faces were completely unclimbable.

The second cataract was really a long and furious rapid—class six; impossible.

In each case a portage was unavoidable, Bolan carrying his kayak and Bjornstrom humping the deflated Hypalon raft, with both men returning each time to fetch the outboard engine, which they maneuvered over the fissured rock between them.

Afloat again, and making good time toward Grimsstadir, they saw the same monoplane Bolan had twice before recognized, low beyond a bluff overlooking the river. But this ship came out of the thickening dusk in the north, not from the hilly ramparts buttressing the ancient crater.

"Keeping tabs," Bolan called to the Icelander. "My guess, once they've located us again, is some kind of surface attack at dawn, just before we pack it in for the day."

Whatever else could be said about the killers, it had to be admitted they were punctual.

Their own rubber raft, Bolan guessed, must have been off-loaded upriver from a truck. It was a quieter, cleaner and closer method than another helicopter assault. Probably more efficient, too, in the long run.

It wouldn't have been too difficult for them, either, deciding where to make their launch. Between the reach where the spotter plane had last seen them and the Dettifoss—Iceland's largest waterfall, a few miles downstream—there was only one sector where two men and two boats could remain unseen during the daylight hours—a long winding canyon where the river twisted through an extrusion of igneous rock that pierced the lava plateau.

Here frost and biting winds had hollowed huge caves from the cliffs, the rush of icy water below had sculpted granite and other rock that Bolan couldn't recognize into great curving overhangs that resembled petrified waves breaking.

Bolan and his companion were starting to stow their gear and settle down on the shingle beach at the far end of a lofty cavern when they heard the stutter of the Russians' outboard.

There were five men aboard. Two of them carried Czech-made Skorpion machine pistols, another couple were armed with the latest model Uzi submachine guns. The helmsman, minding the engine, wore a webbing harness that supported a row of grenades and a holstered Stetchkin automatic.

Bolan saw them in the distance, veering from side to side of the canyon, checking out each hollow among the tumbled rocks with their weapons at the ready.

"Damn!" Bolan said. "We're finished if we stay here. We'll have to run for it now!"

Bjornstrom carried two spare clips for the Ingram's 30-round magazine. He slammed one in and pushed the inflatable raft back into the water. Bolan's two guns were already loaded. He eased himself into the kayak's cockpit and fastened the spray skirt.

"You want me to tow?" the Icelander asked. "While the river is smooth here I can maybe go faster."

Bolan shook his head. "If there are two of us and they go for both, it cuts their effective firepower by half; if they fix on one, the other will be free to give covering fire and enfilade them."

The Russians were between three and four hundred yards upstream. Bjornstrom jerked the cord, and the Excelsior roared to life while the enemy craft was beached and a pair of hardmen were exploring a long, narrow cave between two slabs of lava that had broken away from the cliff and fallen into the river.

Bolan nosed the kayak into the stream and started paddling furiously; the Icelander also shoved out his raft and scrambled over the inflated side. He lowered the outboard into the water and sat with the tiller in one hand. The Ingram lay ready on the thwart beside him.

There was a shout from the Russians.

Bolan glanced over his shoulder and saw the two recon scouts running back to their craft. He paddled as fast as he could, his arms flailing the paddle in and out of the swirling water. Bjornstrom chugged past, furrowing the surface with white. "There is fast water after the next bend," he shouted. "But I think we make it more quickly than them."

Bolan nodded. No point wasting energy with words.

The fast water was in fact a boiling rapid, where the river hurled itself down a slope interspersed with ragged tips of rock that threatened every second to slit the gray Hypalon of the raft and rip open the kayak's hull.

Bjornstrom cut the engine and tipped fuel tank, shaft and screw out of the racing water as he allowed himself to be carried on by the stream, parrying left and right with forceful strokes of a single concave paddle.

Bolan was wielding his two-blade like a crazy man, bracing every few yards with feet and knees straining against the supports, wrists aching from the leverage necessary to thrust the kayak against the force of the current.

Raft and kayak were more often than not three-quarters submerged among the whitecaps of the wild water as the two men gave everything they had to keep their craft away from the perilous crags.

In the last few yards before the Russians' raft was swept into the rapid, they opened fire.

But small craft half swamped in foam and bobbing like corks made tough targets at two hundred feet. At three hundred yards it was just a waste of ammunition. The rasp of the Uzis was lost in the river's roar; wherever the slugs went, it was nowhere near Bolan or the Icelander.

Beyond the rapid the river widened again and the canyon's rocky walls fell away to reveal a barren moonscape of black gravel and volcanic shale studded with vast blocks of primeval stone. And it was here, where the river ran wide and fairly shallow, that the death squad began gaining on the Executioner and his friend.

Spent slugs splashed just astern of the kayak. Bolan plowed grimly on, sweat streaking his face as he urged the lightweight canoe ever faster ahead of the streaming current. There was no point attempting to return the fire—if the Uzis were out of range it would be senseless to lose ground while he wasted ammunition from his two shorter-range handguns.

Bjornstrom was using the outboard again. The rubber raft, stern squatting in the water, was forging ahead. Twin waves curled outward from the prop to wash up the banks of dark shingle on either side of the river.

Twice the Icelander turned around to loose off a short burst from the Ingram—neither caused any damage to the pursuing raft or its occupants—but most of his effort was concentrated on an island of rumbled stones surrounding a basalt outlier that divided the river into two sections a quarter of a mile ahead.

If he could beach his own boat and get among those rocks while the Russians were still afloat...if he could start shooting in earnest from the cover of those boulders while they were still vulnerable on their raft...if he could make the goddamn island before the bastards were near enough to get Bolan in their sights...

But the Executioner was tiring. He had been using every ounce of his formidable strength for more than two miles, and even he could not keep that up indefinitely.

The hunters were seventy yards away. The stabbing roar of the Uzis and the harsher rasp of Skorpion machine pistols were audible over the sounds of the river. But from the moment their firepower was directed at Bjornstrom.

His raft was fifty yards short of the island...forty... thirty...

And then suddenly the engine sputtered and died. The craft listed heavily to starboard as the rubber gunwale on that side began to deflate. The assassins' bullets, aimed first at the boat rather than the man, had struck home.

The raft spun slowly, deep in the water, moving sluggishly toward the channel, racing past the western side of the island.

Bolan's kayak, losing ground rapidly to the Russians, was on the far side of the river.

The killer craft was less than fifty yards away.

Bjornstrom leaped into the water. Waist deep, he forced his way to shore and flung himself down behind the first group of boulders.

From between two humps of granite he triggered a long burst from the MAC-11, the shots cracking out so fast one after the other that they resembled a continuous deadly drumroll.

One of the Russians dropped his Uzi into the river and folded forward over the inflated gunwale with a flood of crimson spurting from his savaged chest. Blood oozed out between his clenched fingers. But the other SMG was still shooting at the island. Bjornstrom was forced to duck to avoid a hail of lead splatting off the rocks on either side.

The men with the Skorpions were both firing at Bolan now. A squad of steel-jacketed skull busters struck one of the paddle blades and sheared it off as easily as a wire passing through cheese; a second group drilled through the kayak's hull on the waterline. Bolan felt one slice off the heel of his boot as water jetted into the cockpit.

But now suddenly, entering a narrowing channel on the east side of the island, where the current was far stronger, the kayak was seized by the speeding river and whirled away, faster than Bolan could have paddled, toward another wide bend in the river.

In the grip of the same accelerating flow, the pursuers' craft began to spin. The wounded helmsman was unable to hold it straight with his undamaged hand. Following the kayak, it was whisked past the island.

Bjornstrom stood up, scrambled to the top of the central rock pile and discharged the Ingram's magazine. He crouched there, a powerful figure amidst a thin blue haze of gun smoke and the glint of ejected brass shell cases, coolly aiming at the receding Russians.

Bolan was also firing now. Allowing the kayak to chart its own course, he slipped one hand beneath the spray skirt and came up with the Beretta. One after the other, he mailed a succession of triple death wishes the enemy's way, special delivery.

There was confusion on the Russian raft. The remaining Uzi was shooting rearward at Bjornstrom. One of the Skorpions was attempting to change places with the injured helmsman; the other, spraying death Bolan's way, looked over his shoulder and started to shout, pointing now frenziedly downstream. The raft rocked dangerously.

Swinging around the bend in the river, Bolan looked up from the Beretta . . . and saw why the guy was frantic, why the current was speeding up so much. They were fast approaching the Dettifoss.

Centered on a vast plain of naked lava, the waterfall was shaped like a miniature Niagara.

The wide river slid smoothly over a U-shaped shelf in a roaring curtain of white to plummet into a boiling caldron of foam from which the spray rose above the cascade in a misty cloud that veiled the sky.

No man, with or without life jacket or flotation vest, could survive in that hellhole of stormy water, even if by some miracle he survived the dizzying drop.

Bolan dug the half paddle that remained to him feverishly into the current, striving to turn the kayak and face back upstream. But the little craft was becoming waterlogged. Low in the water, it was difficult to maneuver.

And now that the Russians had outdistanced Bjornstrom, all their firepower was concentrated on the canoe.

The chatter of the outboard rose to a crescendo as the new helmsman pulled out maximum power to combat the manic force of the river sucking him toward the murderous cataract. The most he could do was steady the raft while the two gunners, one Uzi and one Skorpion, spat hate in Bolan's direction. Even so, slowly but relentlessly, they were being drawn back toward the fall.

Bjornstrom's swamped and half-deflated raft swept past and disappeared over the edge of the cataract.

Bolan was in the worst position. With half a paddle, he was no match for the mighty force of the rushing water. Steadily, inexorably, the kayak was drawn stern-first toward the lip of the falls.

The Beretta's magazine was empty. Bolan thought he might have winged the remaining submachine gunner, who had flopped down into one of the raft's seats. But he might have been paddling on the far side to help the guy at the tiller. There was no time to check: the wounded killer was firing the Stetchkin with his good arm; the remaining man with the Skorpion—firing from the shoulder with the machine pistol's wire stock extended—was pumping 7.65 mm slugs on full-auto at the kayak.

Seeing the line of holes creep along the prow toward the cockpit, Bolan took advantage of the only maneuver open to him—he swept the paddle blade to one side, snapped his hips violently sideways and dumped the canoe into an Eskimo roll.

The waterlogged canoe turned slowly onto its back; Bolan disappeared beneath the surface.

In the distance, Bjornstrom watched aghast as the keel line of the American's capsized craft was riddled from stem to stern by the Russian gunners. Half awash in the speeding flood, the kayak did not right itself. With increasing speed, it shot toward the lip of the falls.

For a dizzy moment it seemed to hang at the edge, the pointed bow rising almost vertically from the water. Then it vanished into the maelstrom below.

For an instant the Icelander thought he saw Bolan's yellow helmet reappear among the turbulent eddies racing toward the lip, then it, too, was swept away and dropped out of sight.

10

Gunnar Bjornstrom scrambled down from the rock out-crop and leaped into the river. He was a strong swimmer. And he was wearing a life jacket. Even so the turbulent current carried him two hundred yards downstream before he could make the west bank of the Jokulsa a Fjollum.

He was no longer in danger from the Russians. They were too busy trying to avoid death by drowning.

In their eagerness to eliminate the Executioner, they had allowed their raft to drift too near the cataract. Now, even with the outboard engine bellowing at full power, they were losing ground. Frantically they pushed the first gunner Bjornstrom had killed out of the inflatable.

The body was quickly carried away by the current. It vanished into a seething suckhole, reappeared nearer the falls. On the very lip, a leg appeared above the surface, then a limp arm, as if waving in mock farewell. Seconds later it had gone.

The killers were tossing overheard yet another corpse—the second Uziman, who must after all have been wasted by Bolan's final burst. Back at the tiller again, the guy with the shattered arm was screaming hysterically. His two compan-ions took up paddles and began, grim faced, to stroke as hard as they could. But the current's grasp on the raft was relentless—with a terrible inevitability it backed up toward the edge.

Bjornstrom watched the Russians die.

The end was unexpectedly sudden. A brusque acceleration, as if a retaining spring had snapped—or the river had tired of playing cat and mouse and decided to get it over with—and the raft surged toward the deadly lip.

Tilting up as it went over, it hurled out at least two of the occupants before it fell. For an instant Bjornstrom heard their death screams. After that there was nothing but the roar of thousands of tons of water pounding down on the rocks below.

Bjornstrom ran to a narrow pathway cut from the rock on the western margin of the cataract. Spume from the thundering falls had blown across to slick the black rock, and he had difficulty keeping his feet on the slippery, treacherous surface. But at last he arrived on a ledge lower down, from which he could overlook the giant basin hollowed by the water.

There was nothing to see through the spray but the foaming white wilderness into which the great curving curtain of the cascade was plunging.

It was not until twenty minutes later that the hellhole relinquished the first of its prizes—fragments from Bolan's kayak. The spray skirt, a broken paddle, burst-open provision sacks and a portion of the foredeck were spewed out to swirl away on the surface of the river as it raced toward the ocean. Soon afterward the yellow helmet bobbed to the surface, floated into an eddy and was beached on a gravel strip fifty yards downstream. There was no sign of the Russians or their raft.

With a heavy heart, Bjornstrom hurried on. Grimsstadir was five miles away, but he was well-known in the area. And well liked, which is all-important in thinly populated regions. He completed the last three and a half miles on a borrowed pony.

The little town was at the foot of two sheer bluffs facing each other across the Jokulsa a Fjollum valley. Most of the houses set in neat garden plots between each row of streets were of the same style—orderly white rectangles with dormer windows on the upper floors that projected from roofs colored red, green, terra-cotta or midnight blue. Bjorn strom passed them all and went into an older building at one side of a square, a gray stone pile that housed the local commissariat of police.

THE MOMENT HE HAD DUMPED the crippled kayak into the first part of an Eskimo roll, Bolan made what expert paddlemen called a "wet exit." He ripped off the spray skirt, released his helmet and dived out of the cockpit. He was at once seized by the current and rolled away from the capsized canoe.

Ten yards downstream there was a suckhole five feet across and probably half as deep again. Bolan was swept underwater toward this swirling funnel and held down beneath the surface by the hydraulic pressure of the stream.

It was surprisingly clear down there. He could make out every detail of the freckled granite boulder submerged just below the surface, which created the miniwhirlpool; he could see the smooth, dark bedrock at the bottom of the river; he could see farther on the stone-layered face of a shelf that formed a rampart between him and the lip of the falls.

If he could make that rampart and stay submerged below it, there was a chance that he could work his way to the east bank of the river and get out. And if not...

He had two alternatives, both lethal—he would remain spinning in the suckhole and drown, or he would float above the level of the rampart and be swept instantly over the edge of the cataract.

Bolan knew that the only way to escape the deadly clutch of a suckhole was down. He knew there would be a wave above the rampart that would marginally reduce the strength of the current on that part of the river.

He jerked the quick-release toggle of his buoyancy vest and swam powerfully down under the vortex to the undercurrent. At once he was whirled away from the suckhole, his face inches from the rocky bed, and then shot to the surface like a cork.

He gasped a single lungful of air and dived again, thrusting deep with all his strength. He was perilously near that tall wave, and beyond it there was nothing but the lip, nothing to stop him being shot over into the seething maelstrom below.

He was above the rock rampart now, still shooting downstream.

An extra push of his legs . . . a desperate grab for a rough projection as he wedged the fingers of his other hand into a crevice splitting the chiseled face...and then slowly, against the manic force of the current, he hauled himself down until he was crouched on the riverbed in the shelter of the rampart.

He lay flat, pressing himself into the angle between rock and riverbed, and started to crawl toward the bank.

It was a difficult maneuver. He had to concentrate on forward movement, yet combine this with resistance to the lateral pull of the current that threatened every second to pluck him away from his underwater refuge and hurl him into oblivion.

The sounds of the river were drowned by the roaring of blood in his ears, the rattle of stones by the thump of his heart. He had no idea how far he had crawled or how far he had still to go.

He was running out of air; his lungs were bursting with the effort of moving in an oxygen-deprived situation.

Bolan forced himself onward. He had forgotten the purpose of his vacation trip, forgotten the mystery of the river, the Russians and Bjornstrom, forgotten even the risk of hurtling over the falls to his death. Every fiber of his being was centered on a single aim—to reach the riverbank before his lungs gave out on him and he lost consciousness.

Or died.

For although Bolan was an athlete, a man with a husky body never less than one hundred percent in shape, he had always preferred to pit his agility, speed and muscular coordination, his strength and determination against the forces of nature rather than those of a human competitor.

"The only meaningful competition," he wrote once in his journal, "is against oneself. But perhaps competition is not the right word—it is more that one pushes oneself to the ultimate limits of endurance, capacity and capability and, in coming back from these limits, learns a lesson more valuable than any to be gained besting another person."

It was this ethos that had brought him to Iceland in the first place, this which urged him to continue his challenge even after the Russians had organized a manhunt placing his life in jeopardy.

And in the end it was Bolan's particular brand of steely determination that triumphed over adversity. But it was a near thing, a very near thing.

Into his dimming consciousness floated the idea that the face of the rock rampart was losing height, that the pull of the current had diminished, that the water was shallower.

With the last of his fading strength he dragged himself a final few yards... and let go.

He sat up on the bed of the river.

And his head was above water.

Bolan gulped in great drafts of air, breathing in ragged gasps until the hammering of his heart slowed down. He sat without moving, staring out across the swirling surface of the river, the crashing roar of the waterfall once more in his ears.

There was no sign of the Russians or their raft. The water flowed remorselessly onward, hurling itself over the lip of the cataract. He saw Bjornstrom running along the far bank, but for the moment he was too weak to call out. In any case his voice would have been lost in the thunder of the falls.

By the time he staggered to his feet and waded ashore, the Icelander was no longer in sight.

Bolan knew roughly how far he was from Grimsstadir. For direction, all he had to do was follow—at a discreet distance, because the Russians would be back—the course of the river. But right now the idea of a five-mile march across that bleak, inhospitable lava plain held little attraction for him.

He had been paddling all night—and most of the previous day, when lack of suitable cover, plus the fight with the hoods in the chopper, had cheated him of his rest. He realized, and the heaviness of his overtaxed limbs confirmed it, that he had slept for only one four-hour stretch since he lowered himself into the sinkhole on the Vatnajokull glacier.

If he was to retain the cutting edge of his reactions, the split-second timing that his dangerous trade demanded, he must rest up. Soon.

Before he rolled the kayak, Bolan had stuffed the Beretta back in the waterproof pouch along with his AutoMag. This, with another neoprene sack, was still clipped to his belt.

Tightly wrapped in that second container were thermal inners and the skintight blacksuit that had become the Executioner's trademark. There was also a folded, ultralight-weight plastic sack that could be opened out to the size of a small suitcase.

Bolan stripped off his wet rubbers and exercised his lithe, muscular body in the chill northern air until his skin was dry. He dressed quickly in the cellular inners, pulled on the blacksuit and packed the pouch containing his weapons, his holstered combat belt and the wet suit into the plastic case. It closed with a nylon zipper and sported reinforced handles.

Three hundred yards below the falls, a bluff rose on the eastern side of the river with boulders scattered along the foot of the rock face. Bolan found a sheltered crevice between two of these, lay down with his head resting on the plastic sack and slept.

HE WOKE AS THE LIGHT FADED and continued on his way to Grimsstadir.

So far, no clear plan had formed in his mind. He would keep following the Russians, for sure. But now that the kayak was gone, organization of any precise details relating to the chase would have to be played by ear. There was money zippered into his belt. Perhaps he could rent another boat at Grimsstadir.

He knew, too, that Bjornstrom had survived the dangers of the waterfalls. But whether or not the big Icelander would rejoin him was no more than a question mark.

Whatever, he would play the cards the way he always did, the way they were dealt.

What astonished him this time was the joker he found in his hand.

The last half mile of his journey to the silent, shuttered town was along a paved highway. Before the first houses there was a gas station with a single pump. He was striding silently past when a voice whispered from the shadows behind the pump.

"Mr. Mack Bolan?"

The warrior stopped in midstride, hairs prickling on the nape of his neck. His guns were still inside the plastic carrier.

"Who wants to know?" he said huskily.

"A friend. I have a gift for you from Gunnar."

Bolan's taut muscles relaxed. It couldn't be a trap—there was no way the Russians could have known the identity of the second fighter who had downed their chopper. "Advance, friend," he said dryly, shades of army guard duty flooding his memory, "and be recognized."

He caught his breath. The figure stepping out from behind the pump was that of a woman. As far as he could see in the half light she was tall, slim and blond. Her features were in shadow, but he could see that her hair was cut very short, that she wore jeans and a sweater . . . and, yeah, that she was stacked.

Most surprising of all was the "gift" that she held out to him without another word.

It was a Heckler & Koch G-11 caseless assault rifle.

11

The Heckler & Koch G-11 looks more like a carrying case for some esoteric musical instrument than a death machine. The twenty-nine-inch grooved plastic housing has no protuberances and only two holes—the muzzle and an opening for ejecting misfired rounds. The pistol grip beneath is at the exact center of gravity and the carrying handle above it also acts as an optical sight.

The rate of fire is very high—two thousand rounds per minute maximum, but this is reduced to six hundred on normal autofire.

Although the one hundred rounds contained by the weapon are only 4.7 mm caliber they can be fired in 3-round bursts each lasting only ninety milliseconds and each capable of piercing a steel helmet at a range of five hundred yards.

Mack Bolan was familiar with the gun and its capability. In the present circumstances it was a welcome gift, particularly if there was going to be any action underwater. But its arrival, and the manner of that, was as mysterious as the rest of the events of the past few days.

"I don't understand," he said. "Who are you? How come Gunnar knew I would be here on this road at this time?"

Her name, she told him, was Erika Axelsson. She was a friend of Bjornstrom's. He was aware of her smile in the dawn light. "It was not so difficult. Gunnar thought at first you had been drowned at the Fjallagfoss. He was very sad. But later one of the Fokker coast-guard planes reported a man sleeping between rocks on the banks of the Jokulsa a Fjollum, and he guessed that it could be you.''

Bolan shook his head in bewilderment. He must have been beat, all right—he hadn't even heard the plane.

''After that,'' Erika continued, ''well, he said he knew you must come to town. He knew you would probably make it at night. This is the only road you could come by.''

''Yeah, but he didn't know—he couldn't have known— what time I'd arrive. I didn't know myself.''

''That was not so much a problem. All I had to do was wait. I have been here since midnight,'' the woman said simply.

''You waited for me all night?'' Bolan was astonished. ''Well, I am grateful. But I don't get it. What's your angle? For that matter, what's his?''

''Excuse me?''

''I mean . . . well, why are you doing this?''

''I told you. I am his friend.''

''Okay. But people don't hang in around deserted gas stations all night toting this kind of thing.'' He hefted the assault rifle in both hands. ''I mean, you have to agree it's a little . . . unusual.''

''Gunnar is an unusual man.''

''Yeah, I found that out. Luckily for me, too. He says he's mad at the Russians for screwing around in his country and he wants to find out why. But that can't be the whole story. What is he really? Some kind of cop?''

''You will have to ask Gunnar,'' Erika said.

Bolan grinned. ''I already did. I didn't get very far. But I'll keep at it. I don't give up that easy.''

''Gunnar, also. He is a very determined man. But sometimes even for such men it is necessary to trust people, trust them without knowing everything.''

"Sure it is," Bolan said. "I think your friend Gunnar and me proved that. Still, even with someone you trust, there are times when it would help to know just who you are trusting!"

But he could pry nothing more from the woman—about herself, about Bjornstrom or about the special, secret interest he showed in the Russian intrigue.

Bolan sighed. As soon as he located one piece of the puzzle and locked it into place, another sector blanked out on him.

"Gunnar asked that you should wear these," Erika said. She ducked back into the shadows and produced baggy sailcloth pants, a fisherman's sweater and a battered watch cap with a shiny peak. "He will meet you at the lakehead at midday. You will find him by the small jetty, in a rubber dinghy with the motor outside, you know?"

"Whatever you say." Bolan drew the clothes on over his blacksuit. He was past asking questions. He had told himself he would play the cards the way they were dealt. So okay, here was a fresh hand, straight out of the shoe. "What do I do between now and midday?"

"There is a place near the lake. Sometimes tourists can be there, foreigners who fish or men interested in the . . . in the rocks, yes?"

"Geologists?"

"Yes. Geologists. You can look at the rocks, too. Or walk by the water. At this season, nobody will ask questions. But first you can come into the town and drink coffee—for the lake you must go to the intersection on the far side of Grimsstadir and then turn left for the main road to the bridge. It is perhaps three miles in all."

Bolan had finished dressing. The sky was lightening. It would soon be full daylight. "We go now," the girl said. "I will show you the coffee place, then I must leave you."

Suddenly she reached up and touched his face. "You are a strong man," she said. "Like Gunnar. I like a man that he should be strong and brave." Seeing Bolan's expression, she gave a little laugh. "You are not shocked? In my country we have a tradition— a girl is not afraid to say if she likes a man."

"In your country?" The phrase had slipped out, Bolan thought, as though she, too, was a foreigner in Iceland. "Don't you come from this part of the world then?"

Erika evaded a direct answer. "It was a manner of speaking," she said. "Come. We must be quick now." She began walking toward the center of town.

Bolan was intrigued nevertheless. "What about Gunnar?" he queried, hurrying to keep up with her. "Doesn't he mind when you . . . say that you like another man?"

"Why should he? Gunnar is a friend. We work together sometimes. Sometimes we may play."

Yeah, Bolan thought. But what's the name of the game? What business are these characters in?

Clearly there was nothing more to be gained from the blonde. He glanced at her face as they approached a small square where shopkeepers were already setting out sidewalk stalls of fruit and vegetables. Small nose, wide mouth, square, determined chin. Eyes that were very blue beneath the pale, cropped cap of hair. The kind of girl who knew exactly what she wanted. And would make damned sure that she got it.

He watched her walking away along a narrow street after she had pointed out a café where workingmen cradled cups of steaming coffee behind the misted windows. Seeing the rounded swell of breasts beneath the tight sweater, the supple curves of hip and thigh as she moved, he experienced a sudden pang of desire, a fleeting wish that he really was still on vacation, free to use his leisure time any way he wanted. He looked at the woman's retreating figure again. Later, there might be time.... For him, romance would have to wait until he found some answers to the present mystery.

Every fiber of his being was dedicated to that end.

Bolan strode out beyond the town with the caseless assault rifle concealed in his plastic carryall.

After the intersection, the road arrowed across a stony stretch of moorland to the bridge at the lakehead. Here, for the first time since he left Egilsstadir, Bolan saw automobiles and trucks. There were not many; most of the cars were old, local three-cylinder Saabs, battered Volvos dating back to the 1950s, Volkswagen Beetles. The trucks were mainly small, loaded down with crates of produce, and he remembered that, despite the near-polar latitude, long daylight hours permitted the cultivation of tomatoes, peaches and sometimes even bananas grown in greenhouses.

He noticed the Renault panel truck not because it lacked lettering along its sides, not even because it was new and carried Reykjavik license plates, but because of a slight hesitation in its approach, a momentary pause in the even note of the engine as it drew abreast. As if the driver was satisfying himself that he had arrived in the right street, at the correct address.

Or that the person he was passing was the one he sought.

Bolan had the impression of heavyset men—he couldn't tell their numbers—crowded into the truck. Men dressed in anonymous gray. Then it accelerated, sped up a slight rise and vanished into the dip beyond.

The Executioner continued his unhurried pace. But the zipper of the plastic holdall was open now and his right hand was already inside, wrapped around the pistol grip of the G-11.

He saw the panel truck slewed across the road at the bottom of the depression as he breasted the rise. There was no other traffic in sight. Two men were crouched behind the hood. Two more were running for clumps of stone at each side of the road. A fifth appeared between the open rear doors of the truck. All of them were armed with submachine guns.

Bolan didn't wait for them to fire first. Maybe they had orders simply to get the drop on him and bring him in alive for questioning. At any rate the SMGs did not open up the moment his head and shoulders appeared in view.

The Executioner flung himself to the side of the roadway, finger tight around the Heckler & Koch's trigger. Fired from inside the plastic suitcase, the gun spewed out a blaze of death that ripped through the fifty yards separating Bolan from the truck so quickly that the killers behind the hood died before they had a chance to shoot. The diminutive 4.7 mm rounds drilled through metal, mangled pipes and hoses and wiring, and cored through human flesh. A cloud of blood sprayed through the air as the hardmen fell.

By the time the three others opened fire, Bolan was prone on the hill, his body shielded by the stone heaps.

Flame spurted from between the truck's open rear doors. Hollowpoint death bringers scuffed the tarmac at the roadside and whistled through the coarse grass above the ditch.

Bolan jerked the G-11 from the carryall, snuffed out the smoldering edges where the gun's muzzle-flashes had melted the plastic, and fired again.

He stitched a double line of destruction hip-high across the doors. The gunner crumpled to the ground, with northern daylight showing through his skull.

Two hitmen remained in the ditches.

Bolan dropped the case, leaped to his feet and sprinted across to the far side of the road with the H&K.

A stream of slugs struck sparks from the granite chips in the pavement as he ran. But the gunman on the far side had revealed his position. Flattening himself behind the opposite stone pile, Bolan hammered another burst low down through the moorland sedge. Small clods of earth fountained into the air and spattered the roadside. He heard a strangled scream. In the far ditch something flopped briefly among the grasses and then lay still. There were no more shots from that side of the highway.

Four down and one to go. Bolan crawled stealthily along the depression, inching his way downhill in the hope of seeing the last killer before he had a chance to fire. Figuring he could finish it with a single blast, the guy stood upright with a grenade in his hand.

He hadn't reckoned with Bolan's split-second reactions—or the G-11's rate of fire. Bolan caught him with the full force of a half-second burst when his arm was still drawn back to throw. The bomber collapsed into a huddle of blood-stained rags. The grenade flew from his hand and exploded harmlessly on the upland turf near the truck. Shattered glass tinkled to the roadway.

Bolan rose to his feet, replaced the assault rifle in the damaged plastic holdall and walked to the truck. The engine refused to start—carburetor, feed pipes and inlet manifold had been mangled by the G-11's first murderous eruption. He pushed it into the ditch, hauled the bodies into the rear section, closed the doors and continued on his way. He was in sight of the lake before the next vehicle passed him on the way to Grimsstadir.

Bjornstrom arrived punctually at midday at the tiller of a Hypalon raft exactly like the one he had lost at the Fjallagfoss.

But this one carried large white numerals painted on the inflated gunwales.

It was clearly some kind of official craft.

Another section of the puzzle clicked into place. "I get it," Bolan said. "This guy from the Icelandic Water Board, the inspector you say checks out the pump houses and the pipelines 'once in a while,' that's you, am I right?"

Bjornstrom nodded.

"And you found out that the Russians were tapping your supply and decided to carry out a more detailed... inspection...on your own?"

"That is correct."

"But why? Why not just tip off your bosses? Why not call in the army or the police or whatever? Tell these bastards where they get off."

"There is no army," Bjornstrom said. "As for the police, it would require action at diplomatic level. The real reasons could be buried—or the plot abandoned and restarted a different way. I prefer first to find out the truth. Then, maybe, when we know what the project is, it can be stopped."

"Okay," Bolan said, "I understand that. But...are Ingrams and G-11s part of your normal inspector's kit?"

"Absolutely," the Icelander joked. "I got dozens of them. I give them to my friends at Christmas!"

"And the girl? Erika?"

"She is a friend."

And the Executioner had to be content with that unsatisfactory answer once more.

Bjornstrom started the outboard, and they nosed out into the lake. It was in fact no more than a sinuous drowned valley gashing the bare landscape, dammed at the far end by a shelf of harder rock. Its narrow, fifteen-mile length was dotted with small islands, but they saw very few boats—most of them were solitary fishermen—and nobody fired on them from above the walls of the canyon.

Beyond the natural dam, the Jokulsa a Fjollum thundered down beneath a dense cloud of spume into Iceland's largest, deepest, widest cataract, the Dettifoss. Three miles farther on the two men were faced with a shorter but no less arduous portage on account of a smaller waterfall called the Rettarfoss.

After that, the stream wider and slower now, there were bleak lowlands to cross, high ground to the east with the fifteen-hundred-foot smoking cone of Pristikluvatn, one of the island's many active volcanoes, and at last the division of the river into several branches that ran out into the great northern bay named the Axarfjordur.

The trip took them two days.

They passed beneath the bridge near the Russian concession exactly one week after Bolan had driven over it on his way from Akureyri to Egilsstadir.

He looked at the surface workings a lot more closely this time.

They crested a ridge that separated the steep-sided fjord from a smaller arm of the sea that pierced the indented coastline to the west. The narrow neck of land between these two inlets was blanked off by a ten-foot wall approached by a winding mountain track.

"The gates are guarded by men with shotguns," Bjornstrom said, "and there are dog handlers with Doberman pinschers patrolling the perimeter."

The ridge, isolated in this way as much as an island, was leased in its entirety to the Russians, he told the Executioner. The tin roofs of pithead buildings were half hidden by a swell of moorland, but the twin wheels of the colliery-style hoist on their iron pylons were clearly visible against the gray sky.

"What exactly are they supposed to be mining?" Bolan asked.

Bjornstrom shrugged. "Prospecting actually. Tin lodes, veins rich in other minerals, certain ores among the granites and quartzites that form the promontory. Uranium, for all I know. Enough, anyway, to make a believable reason for having surface plant, bore-sinking equipment, the pithead gear that you can see and a shaft with a cage."

"And at the foot of the shaft?"

"That is what we have to find out."

"Any chance of scaling that cliff?" Bolan jerked his head toward the seamed rock face that lay between the coarse grass on top of the ridge and the deep water of the fjord.

"It is possible, but guards patrol all the time. We better can make some entry through the caves."

"Caves?"

Bjornstrom cut the engine and allowed the raft to drift. "If I go farther, they may suspect. We inspect as far as the bridge, where the river becomes tidal."

"You mentioned caves?"

"Yes. This site is well chosen. By road, the nearest village is seven miles away. In a direct line, the nearest is Pvera, on the other side of the fjord." He pointed at the opposite cliff. Some way farther north, slate roofs and chimneys could be seen on the skyline. "But to get there by road is twice as far."

"The caves!" Bolan insisted.

The Icelander pointed seaward once more, this time below the ridge on which the concession was located. A grass-topped spur jutted out from the cliff and curled around toward them. "The spur is granite," he said. "It is weathered in blocks and cubes, which makes climbing easier. But there is also a basalt dike by the fault that separates the spur from the ridge, and that runs out underwater like a jetty."

Bolan waited patiently.

"Between these two," Bjornstrom said, "there are three caves. The openings above the surface are high enough to allow a rowing boat to enter at high water, a larger craft when the tide is low."

"And you figure there may be a connection between these caves and the mine shaft?" At last Bolan permitted himself to show eagerness at the thought of something positive.

"It is possible," Bjornstrom said. "Dressed this way, we are believable—as Water Board officials—as far as the bridge. To go farther, unless we are fishing or in a coast-guard cutter, could alert the guards above.''

"So we wait until dark?"

"I think so. As you see, curving this way, that bluff cuts off the view of the caves from anyone across the fjord in Pvera. That could work for us, too. So I say we forget about being Water Board inspectors and go tonight, as ourselves, swimming, to see about those caves. Okay?"

"You got it," Bolan said.

THE WATER WAS COLD as sin, black as a starless night in the south. It wrapped icy fingers around heart and lungs as if it would squeeze every vestige of life away, plastering the wet suits to their bodies so close that the insulating film of moisture was almost neutralized.

Bolan led the way, swimming strongly in a modified Australian crawl that left scarcely a ripple on the dark surface of the fjord. They had paddled the raft silently to a diminutive creek two hundred yards upstream and left it behind a granite outcrop that rose from the water. On this initial recon they were equipped with flippers, face masks, snorkel tubes and electric lamps brow-strapped above the masks. A commando knife was the only weapon each man carried.

They didn't need to use the lamps.

Bolan was not surprised. During the afternoon, hidden among rocks a quarter of a mile away, they had heard unmistakable sounds of activity within the caves. And if there was work, there might be light.

Noises carried clearly along the surface of the fjord, and the Executioner could distinguish the tapping of rock chisels, a scrape of metal, the noise of a distant compressor and even, from time to time, the swish of a concrete mixer. Once he thought he heard guttural commands. Then whistles blew and there was silence . . . followed by five small but distinct explosions.

"Blasting," Bolan said. "Between the whistle and the detonation, they all take shelter someplace. It might be a good time to get in there."

Bjornstrom nodded. "And find a place to hide before they come out again and start to work?"

"Right. There has to be a physical connection between the bore they are sinking up top and those caves. If we can hear these noises, so can people from Pvera and boatmen in the fjord. So the Russians must have a plausible reason for blasting and whatever else they do at the foot of the mine shaft."

"Galleries radiating out from there?" Bjornstrom suggested.

"Yeah. But that can't be the real reason, or there'd be no need for them to try and eliminate guys like you and me. My guess is that it's the caves themselves are the target—they're up to something big inside those caves that they want to keep secret—and the mine shaft beyond them is just a cover, to account for the noise."

"What do you mean, 'something big'?"

"Beats me. I've been racking my brains for days trying to think up a believable reason. Now that I'm sure it's connected with the river and these caves, I'm as much in the dark as ever. Some kind of clandestine propaganda broadcasting unit? A KGB disaffection HQ? Antimissile detection? A military launchpad? None of those makes any sense at all. Not in caves. And certainly not in Iceland."

"So okay, we find out more when we go in," Bjornstrom said.

Before they started to swim, the sky darkened and rain pelted the fjord from the ocean. By the time they were halfway to the cave mouths it had changed to a sea mist—a damp curtain of gray that rolled quickly across the water, settling a thin layer of moisture on rock faces, distorting sounds and blotting out shapes on both sides of the inlet.

They surfaced thirty yards offshore and stared at the cave mouths. The top of the cliff, which rose sheer from the fjord, was hidden in the mist. The far side of the fjord was invisible; there was no conceivable place where a lookout could be posted above or beside the caves. "We can take our time," Bjornstrom said.

In the gathering dusk a subdued radiance escaped from the largest of the three openings, which looked to be about forty feet wide and seven or eight high. One of the others was almost as far across but the roof was only just above the surface. The third was much smaller.

Bolan pushed up his mask. "That could be the safest way in for us," he said, indicating the third cave. "Providing they interconnect."

He swam nearer. The rock bordering the openings was weathered, cracked and split by frost, eroded by wind and salt and then worn smooth by millennia of waves and storms and spray. "I'm going on in and check the entrance," he murmured. "You stick around here as end stop, okay?"

Bjornstrom nodded. Bolan readjusted his mask, dived beneath the surface and disappeared.

The Icelander swam around in circles for a few minutes to keep his circulation active. The remorseless pressure of the icy water numbed his fingers and toes, created an ache in the pit of his stomach. Finally, he, too, submerged and propelled himself underwater as far as the spur.

He pulled himself up onto a granite shelf and investigated the state of the rock. As far as he could see in the waning light, an experienced climber could easily hoist himself up to a height of about twenty feet—and from there, along a fissure splitting the age-old face, he could cross to the cliff directly above the caves.

The quartzite there was seamed by a number of horizontal stratifications that formed narrow ledges above the openings, but whether or not there was any way of gaining the interior from these—or whether that could be done unobserved—he was in no position to see.

The subdued light from the main cave was not reflected in the black water of the fjord, but the channel inside must have curved, or perhaps there was some trick of the light, for he could see nothing but a pale blur beyond the arch.

An instant later he saw nothing at all. Silently from behind, a sinewy steel-hard forearm locked beneath his jaw, clamping his throat in a viselike grip. At the same time hard fingers probed the rubber helmet behind his ear, searching for the pressure point that would paralyze him.

Bjornstrom struggled wildly, clawing at the forearm, striving to shake free of the hand clasped around the base of his skull. He gagged, choking for air. His feet scrabbled on the granite ledge; fragments of rock tore free and splashed into the water below.

The darkness threatening to engulf him turned red. He felt the strength seep from his limbs . . . and then suddenly the iron grasp on his throat relaxed. His head was free. He heard a choking cry as the air wheezed back into his own tortured lungs, and he fell to the ground.

Mack Bolan was standing above him, supporting the limp figure of his attacker. Bolan's knife had arrowed in between the man's teeth and penetrated the roof of his mouth, transfixing the lower part of the brain and killing him instantly.

The Executioner withdrew the flat blade and tipped the body over the ledge into the water below before the blood cascading down the guy's gray combat fatigues stained the rock.

"With luck he'll be washed clean before he's found," Bolan said quickly. "The palate wound will not register unless they're looking for it. The marks on the ledge here should indicate that he missed his footing in the fog, fell over and drowned." He pulled the Icelander to his feet and waved aside his thanks. "You weren't to know they'd post a guard out here in this kind of weather," he said. "Do you feel up to making a short recon trip? Underwater?"

"Sure," Bjornstrom croaked, massaging his bruised throat. "What did you find?"

"Well, the caves do connect. We can get to the main cavern through any of them. Also, the place is enormous inside there. Deep water, too. That main archway must go down at least forty feet below the surface. And there's a hell of a lot of work going on."

"What kind of work?"

"That's what we are going to find out," Bolan said. "Come back in with me and we'll check. We better get some idea of the geography of the place before the guard's absence is discovered."

They slid back into the water and headed for the smallest of the arches.

To Bjornstrom, an interminable time seemed to pass before Bolan signaled that it was safe to surface. They had navigated a curving channel perhaps seventy yards long and joined the main entry, where it opened out into an immense cavern.

It was from this that the light reflected in the fjord had come. Now, treading water at the outer margin of this huge chamber hollowed from the rock, they could see under a blaze of arc lights the extent of the work that had already been secretly completed.

What had once been an irregular underground basin had been widened and transformed into a rectangular dock bordered by concrete quays. Beyond this pool two giant lock gates with sluices blanked off a caisson crisscrossed with scaffolding on which an army of laborers worked. A dry-dock was evidently under construction.

Electric wires and compressor tubes tangled the quay nearest the two intruders, and in the far depths of the cave the shafts of rock drills and boring equipment gleamed. Above these a railed gallery circling three parts of the cavern led to a glassed-in box that was clearly some sort of control room.

Two men carrying submachine guns emerged from a passageway carved from the rock and began patrolling the gallery toward the entrance tunnel.

Bolan touched the Icelander on the arm. They submerged and began swimming back along the main channel leading to the fjord.

There was a lot more to check out but the Executioner had already seen enough to know that at last he held the final section of the puzzle in his mind.

This was no underground base for radio misinformation, no simple KGB disaffection headquarters—what he had been looking at were bombproof Russian submarine pens.

The Russians were building a clandestine underwater naval station beneath the territory of a NATO country.

12

"For the new SSK-class minisubs," Bolan said. "There's space for two in that basin, and a third in the dry-dock."

"Minisubs?" Bjornstrom objected. "You mean those two-man undersea motorboats the Italians developed in the Second World War?"

"Hell, no. Mini in relation to the four- or five-thousand-ton nuclear maxis that are too easy to pinpoint with modern sonar and electronic detectors. The SSKs are 200-ton subs with a crew of only twelve, all-electric engines and a sea-to-sea strike capability of no more than half a dozen short-range nukes."

"Harder to detect, though, than the nuclear-powered ships?"

"Sure. They're silent, the heat emanation is minimal, they are fast—and maneuverable as a pursuit plane."

"So. Better than these so-called factory ships then, for monitoring all the NATO and other Western shipping in the North Atlantic?"

"Uh-huh. Preying on them, too. Acting as a hidden strike force if the Soviets ever decide to unleash a hot war. But they do have one big disadvantage."

Bjornstrom nodded. "The batteries."

"Yeah. Prenuclear subs used electric engines for undersea work, diesels on the surface. The SSKs are too small to carry auxiliary engines—and in any case it would louse up their low profile, write them a bigger signature on the detector screens. But electric motors restrict them to a very short range—each accumulator needs to be recharged every *X* miles or every so-many hours.''

"So from Russian bases, Murmansk, Archangel or even the Baltic, an SSK North Atlantic patrol is not a proposition?''

"Right. It was a pretty smart idea, though, to use Iceland.'' Bolan shook his head in reluctant admiration. "Equidistant from Greenland, the Faroes, Spitsbergen and Norway. Smack in the center of the operations area! They could be in among any NATO concentration, anyplace, within a couple of hours. Even under the ice. And it saves them around a thousand miles each way!''

"But the entry to these caves...?'' Bjornstrom looked dubious. They were sitting in the rubber raft, hidden behind the rocks, waiting for the pale gloom of the sub-Arctic night to establish itself.

"A piece of cake,'' Bolan told him. "The fjord is long— but it's also dark and deep, with a rock bottom and no sand to show up underwater craft in silhouette. An SSK could slip in from the open sea and make the whole journey submerged, including entry to the main cave through that drowned arch. It wouldn't need to surface until it was safely out of sight inside the basin.''

"Then they should be building generators in there as well as maintenance and repair facilities?''

"Damn right, they should. Recharging those accumulators will be the most important part of the deal. My guess is that all the water-tapping you come across is not so much for the heating as for generator turbines. They won't want to siphon off too much current from the normal domestic power supply to the fake mine workings above. People might start to ask questions. So they aim to install their own hydroelectric plant below.''

Bjornstrom was feeding shells into a clip destined for the magazine of his Ingram. "So what do we do?" he asked.

"I have kind of a personal stake in this," Bolan said grimly. "We wage a two-man war and destroy the place. Blow it clear to hell."

"We don't just report it to the government and let them handle it?"

"Uh-huh. Like you said, that makes it a diplomatic issue. You got an international incident, violation of sovereignty. Imagine what a help that would be with the next round of SALT talks coming up! Hell, it would make the East-West situation more unstable than ever and kill any chance at all the talks have of reducing the arms race. Whereas a nice quiet little private raid . . ." He left the sentence unfinished.

Bjornstrom looked relieved. "I agree," he said. "If this base is destroyed anonymously, before it is complete, the Russians cannot complain because they are here building it illegally. And Iceland can say nothing because it will know nothing about it."

"Right," Bolan said. "Nobody kicks up hell if a place that doesn't officially exist is wiped out." He smiled. "So all we have to do now is find ourselves a stack of explosives. You got any quarries around here?"

"I do not think that will be necessary," the Icelander said. He held up his hand. "Listen."

Faintly, approaching from the direction of the village on the far side of the fjord, they could hear the creak of rowlocks.

Soon a small boat materialized out of the gloom. A single figure in a frogman suit stowed the oars as the dinghy glided in among the rocks. Then the new arrival leaped nimbly ashore with a canvas satchel. Even in the mist, Bolan could see it was the woman, Erika. "I hope I have forgotten nothing," she said to Bjornstrom.

"I hope not," Bjornstrom said. Shielding the beam from a pocket torch with one hand, he opened the satchel and laid out the contents.

A handful of crimped detonators, three dozen sticks of C4 plastic explosive, twelve cheap wristwatches, one dozen four-and-a-half-volt flashlight batteries, a tube of super-glue, a small transparent plastic tube containing drawing pins, Scotch tape, copper wire on a cardboard spool and a pair of long-nose pliers with rubber-covered handles.

"Yes," he said. "All is here. Thank you, Erika."

"Okay," Bolan said firmly. "I've let you guys string me along long enough. You may have a cover job with the Icelandic Water Board, Bjornstrom, but don't give me any more of this curiosity-of-a-private-citizen crap. And don't tell me your girlfriend just happened to take all this stuff off the shelf in the local supermarket and walk out with it in a wire basket. Who the hell are you two?"

Bjornstrom and the girl looked at each other. Erika smiled at Bolan in the dusk. "We are working together, all of us. There is no reason why you should not know now," she said.

"I'm all ears," Bolan said.

"Gunnar is an Icelandic citizen. He told you. But his family comes from Norway. I, too," she said simply.

Of course, Bolan thought. That fitted. *In my country... we are not afraid... a manner of speaking...*

"In Norway we are vulnerable, with much sea coast. And sometimes we like to know what is going on with our neighbors, even the friendly ones, especially in the ocean. Not to make a fuss but to find out quietly for ourselves, you know?"

"Are you saying," Bolan said, "that Bjornstrom's some kind of a mole, a sleeper? That both of you work for the Norwegian secret service?"

"Yes," Bjornstrom said.

13

"We go in twice," Bolan said. "Once to get an idea of the full layout, make a plan of the weak points and dope out guard routines; a second time to position the charges."

"Tonight?" Erika asked. "While there is still this fog?"

Bolan shook his head. "The fog helps us get close to the caves, but they stopped work already. No more whistles, no more blasting, no more compressors. I guess they don't dare work a graveyard shift in case it makes the locals curious. You wouldn't expect a normal prospecting crew, interested in mineral lodes, to work all night."

"But if nobody's there...? Isn't this the best time to go in and—?"

"No," Bolan cut in. "The place is too bright. There'll still be guards, in case strangers cruise in from the fjord. And intruders are easier to spot if there's nobody else around. Apart from that, the sentry we wasted will have been missed by now, so they'll be on double alert."

"But in that case—" Bjornstrom began.

"Look, when they're blasting, a whistle blows and the whole team make it to some kind of shelter, right? Between the signal and the blast there's a couple, sometimes three minutes, to allow everyone time to take cover. During that time we go in and find a place to hide. Next time they explode charges, we penetrate farther, make a preliminary recon. Same thing the following day when we place our own charges."

"It seems a big deal, wrecking the whole joint with the plastique we have," Bjornstrom said.

"Depends how we use it," the Executioner replied. "We got twelve detonators, a dozen timers and thirty-six sticks of C4. That means twelve charges of three sticks each, one charge of twenty-five sticks and eleven singles...or anything in between. We decide which once we've had a chance to size up the installations."

"We could arrange more but it would take time."

"Hell, no," Bolan said. "We'll make do with what we have. The important thing is to find the strategic places, where a relatively small charge will do the greatest damage. The judo technique."

Bjornstrom looked dubious.

"Turning your opponent's strength against himself," the Executioner explained. "Blow some moving part when the machinery is actually working, and it'll thresh about and do your work for you. A broken drive shaft can do a hell of a lot of damage—far more than we could with a single stick."

"Okay," the Icelander said. "When do we go in, and how?"

"Tomorrow morning, early. And I reckon your traverse is the best way in for starters."

"But will there not be a guard—or guards—on that spur, like tonight?" Erika queried.

"Probably. Almost certainly. We'll have to neutralize them. That's why I want to use that way in first. The Russkies just might swallow one guy falling off a cliff and drowning, but not two or three. After that, you can bet they'd keep special watch on that particular chunk of rock. So our final visit will have to be underwater."

"In that case," Bjornstrom said, "let us hope the mist will not have lifted."

IT WAS DAMP and cold at dawn. Patches of fog still lay across the calm surface of the fjord and veiled the cliff tops overhead.

The two guards on the spur had been carefully briefed. "You must remember," the KGB colonel in charge of security had told them, "that this is not a *military* installation. We are on foreign ground. We have the right to keep people off this ridge. But a guard mounted army style is counterproductive—it would raise suspicion locally. So you carry slug shotguns, not automatic weapons, and you are in plain clothes. You are examining the rocks, maybe looking for birds to shoot, not acting as sentries. Is that clear?"

Yuri Prokhorov had worked his way down almost to sea level. He had no wish to play soldier in this godforsaken hole anyway. He hated Iceland, he hated the cold, he hated guard duty, he hated the colonel and most of all he hated this specific mass of wet and chilly granite on this mother of a morning. If he was back home in the Georgian Republic of the U.S.S.R., on the marshes of the Rion Delta he really could be shooting birds. It would be warm and sunny, too, and the goddamn birds wouldn't need to migrate.

Suddenly a rowboat appeared out of the fog, nosing in to the spur. There were two big men in it, one blond and the other dark, wearing fishermen's sweaters, seaboots and peaked caps. The dark one stood and reached for a projecting ledge as the boat nudged the rock. He started to hoist himself ashore.

Prokhorov scrambled farther down toward the water level. "You cannot land here," he said roughly. "This is private property."

"That's all right," the dark man said in Russian. "We won't do any damage—we only want to climb twenty feet or so, to that grassy shelf up there. It's a good place for the birds."

"You will be trespassing. You can't land here."

The stranger swung himself up easily until he stood beside the guard. His eyes were a piercing blue. "The ducks are flying south," he said, as if Prokhorov hadn't spoken. "We'll be all right here—you can get a good shot across the water from this spur. They'll be coming in low today because of the fog."

"Get into your boat and go back!" the Russian shouted. "In any case the ducks don't—" He froze, staring down at the boat.

There were no guns in it.

He whirled, reaching for his own shotgun. An iron-hard fist slammed into his solar plexus, choking the breath from his lungs. He folded forward, his mouth open to shout a warning, but no sound forced its way past his savaged diaphragm. At the same time the dark man picked him up as easily as if he had been a child and dropped him over the edge into the fjord.

Bjornstrom was ready. The guard plunged into the water, arms flailing and throat gargling, six feet from the boat. Bjornstrom pushed off the rock face with two hands and slid the boat across the intervening space.

He was leaning over the gunwale as the Russian surfaced, still groaning for air. Bjornstrom placed both hands on the man's head and shoved him under again.

The rowboat rocked as the Russian submerged. Bolan stepped down into it and joined his companion.

Prokhorov came up for the second time. Before he could drag in a lungful of air, Bjornstrom leaned out once more and grabbed the back of his jacket. The Norwegian bunched the cloth in his fists and thrust hard down, holding the drowning man against the rowboat just beneath the surface.

The water swirled and frothed. Bubbles burst. Bolan braced himself against the heaving boat as Bjornstrom re-tained the murderous pressure on the Russian's thrashing figure.

Gradually the frenzied struggles slackened. The bubbles ceased. For Yuri Prokhorov the marshes of the Rion Delta suddenly became very real. And the sun unbelievably bright.

ON THE FAR SIDE of the spur, Mikhail Sujic heard the heavy splash when Prokhorov hit the water. He hurried around a shoulder of rock, unslinging his shotgun. The colonel had told them to be extra cautious. Andreyev's body had been found floating three miles away, and the colonel was not entirely convinced his death had been an accident. There were saboteurs around, and an American terrorist had been seen in the region.

Sujic jumped down onto a lower ledge. And stopped dead.

A helmeted figure in a shining black dry-suit was facing him. He saw from the curves of breast and hip molded by the skintight rubber that it was a girl. She held a Beretta 93-R in her right hand. "Drop the gun," she said quietly.

Sujic dropped it.

Then he had second thoughts. He began walking toward her.

"Stop!" she warned. "Or I'll shoot."

He shook his head. "You dare not," he said. And of course he was right. "You'd have a half a dozen men with SMGs running down that cliff path before I hit the deck. Come on—*you* give me *your* gun. I think we'll take you in for a little questioning." Still walking, he held out his hand.

"Come and get me," Erika Axelsson said.

Sujic had guts. He came. Backing his hunch that she would not shoot, he ran at her—a heavy, thickset man with a bull neck and mean eyes.

Erika dropped the Beretta. Sujic didn't know exactly what happened after that. She reached up and grabbed the hand clawing out toward her, dipped one shoulder, jerked and then swiveled from the hips.

Sujic flew through the air. He dropped over the edge of the shelf, landed on his back on a steep slope with a sickening thump and slid off into the fjord.

Dipping an oar over the stern of the rowboat, Bjornstrom was beside him in a few strokes. They grasped his ankles and held his feet up in the air so that the upper half of his body was immersed. He died quickly, probably without regaining consciousness.

Ten minutes later, Erika was swallowed up in the mist, rowing the boat back to their hiding place, and the two men were perched on the shelf linking the spur with the cliff face above the caves.

"Those guys were probably on a four-hour watch," Bolan muttered. "Work in the cavern had already started when we arrived, but we should have plenty of time for our recon before they're missed."

He tensed as whistles shrilled through the mist. "Okay, Gunnar, this is it!" he said.

Facing the cliff with arms outstretched and toes flexed, he led the way along the shelf toward the caves.

Despite the overhang formed by the roof of the arch, they found handholds and footholds in the weathered rock, ducked into the main cave and inched their way around the curve that hid the inner basin from any watcher on the fjord. By the time the sounds of voices and retreating footsteps had died away, they were clambering over the rail of the gallery that circled the dock.

Beside the control room on the far side of the gallery, a spiral stairway snaked down to the quay. Next to it, in a gray steel housing, was a main transformer flanked by a panel covered with complicated switch gear. "That's target number one," Bolan whispered.

"And number two's not far away," the Icelander replied, pointing to a second chamber that opened off the dock. Fed by one of the smaller entrances from the fjord, this was evidently intended for small craft, for there was a shallow slipway leading up out of the dark water with bays on either side. A rowboat was moored in one of the bays.

And at the back of the slipway, pipes emerged from the rock to curl through a second opening beyond which the massive, humped shapes of generators were visible.

Bolan nodded, mentally noting other vulnerable points that he could see—drain covers, junction boxes, parts of the sluice mechanism. "Anyone in the control room?" he murmured.

Bjornstrom, who was farther along the gallery, craned over the rail. He shook his head. "All in the shelter, I guess. But where is the place for the men who set the charges?"

Bolan indicated a doorway beyond the top of the spiral stairway. An arrow with the Russian characters for the word Shelter pointed to a warren of passageways, which he guessed must eventually connect with the mine shaft sunk from the pithead on the ridge far above them.

Inside this opening there was a glassed-in hutch with slatted steel shutters covering the windows through which they could make out the silhouettes of two men with their backs to the dock basin, looking down into the construction chamber.

One of the men raised his arm. Abruptly a jet of brown smoke boiled up behind the scaffolding. A muffled explosion shook the fabric of the gallery and a shock wave assaulted the intruders' eardrums. Seconds later two more detonations filled the air beneath the arcs clustered below the roof with a fog of rock dust.

Bolan and the Icelander were racing around the gallery toward the control room. By the time the whistles blew for the workers to come out of the shelter, the two invaders were concealed behind a stack of forty-gallon oil drums between the stairway and the transformers.

Now, for the first time, they were able to study the opposition at close quarters.

The Russians working in the cavern fell into three categories. The majority—perhaps twenty-five or thirty—were evidently skilled construction men, hard-bitten, professional, experienced. They emerged from the shelter and filed at once down the stairway to restart work on the caisson, some operating compressors and pneumatic drills, others handling concrete mixers, but most of them around the rock face behind the lock gates.

Among them were half a dozen overseers. Equipped like the workers with steel mining helmets, they were distinguished by white oilskin slickers, white boots and black arm bands each with a red star.

The third party, again perhaps half a dozen men, were of an entirely different type—tough, muscular, with bleak and ruthless expressions on their flat Slavic faces.

These were the guards. They wore jackboots over the same gray fatigues that Bolan knew so well, and each was armed with a Skorpion machine pistol. They had nothing to do with the work in progress but maintained a constant patrol throughout the base.

Two went through to the smaller cave, another couple penetrated the maze of passageways between the basin and the mine shaft, one lounged on the quay, staring down at the laborers in the dry-dock. The last strode to the gallery on the far side from the control room.

"Low-grade KGB material," Bolan whispered. "Rank and file heavies, but dangerous—and efficient. There'll be more of them up top."

The control room remained unoccupied. It was obviously designed to operate the whole complex when it was completed, but for the moment orders were transmitted through loudspeaker relays from the two guys in the armored hut at the entrance to the shelter.

For thirty minutes Bolan and the Icelander watched the activity on the rock face. The guard passed their hiding place three times, but he seemed more interested in the basin below than anything at gallery level.

When he reached the far side for the third time, Bolan raised his head cautiously and peered over the top of the nearest drum. "The two dudes behind the steel shutter are looking the other way all the time," he said quietly. "Down into the chamber. The guard up here scrutinizes the cave with the slipway at the end of his promenade. Nobody uses the control room. What do those facts suggest to you?"

"We invade the control room," Bjornstrom replied, "when everybody's back is turned."

"Yeah. It'll save time when the next whistle blows—plus we can probably wise ourselves up on the eventual operations technique, which should save time when we place the charges."

As soon as the guard turned his back and leaned over the rail again, Bolan and Bjornstrom crawled out from behind the drums, sped noiselessly to the control room and slipped inside.

On the floor, out of sight below the glass windows, Bolan stifled a gasp of astonishment when he saw the complexity of equipment in the small room.

Neatly labeled in Cyrillic lettering he saw multiple banks of switch gear and levers to operate the gates and dams of the lock, controls for the shaft and elevator, the generator turbines and all the pithead mechanism. Plus radar installations, monitor screens, a data-bank terminal, the console for a massive computer and a complete radio transmitting and receiving deck. Above the benches, the wall glittered with dials.

"No problem putting this gear out of commission," Bolan said. "Three well-placed sticks would wreck all of it. But how long is it going to take them to replace it? I think they could be back where they are today by next spring, fully operative by summer. And that just isn't good enough. What we need is some structural damage, something to damage the whole damned base so completely that it can't be repaired at all."

"You mean like blowing a hole in the bottom of the fjord and letting all the water out?" Bjornstrom joked.

"Something like that. Destroying the shaft for a start. And if we could sabotage the entrance in some way..."

"But we could!" Bjornstrom was excited. "Have you noticed the state of the rock when we came in?"

"Yeah, it was weathered to hell. Dangerous too, some of it—rotted enough to crumble away in your hand."

"Something else besides. There is two hundred feet of cliff above the main entrance. This is one big weight to press down on an arch that does not even have a keystone."

"You mean...?" Bolan in turn looked excited.

"I mean there is already a cracking and a partial subsidence. One big slab of granite has slipped and jammed itself across a chimney in the rock face. While it is there, all remains firm. But if it was not there..." Bjornstrom paused and shook his head.

"How much would come down?"

"I am not a professional quarryman, but I think maybe one thousand, two thousand tons."

"Right into the channel leading to the cavern? You mean it could block—or at least partly block—the minisubs' entry?"

The Icelander nodded.

Bolan was jubilant. "And *that* damage they could never repair. They could never clear the passage again because it couldn't be done secretly—the whole world would see what they were doing! Can we get to this slab unseen? Have we enough plastic to dislodge it?''

"We need to fracture only one corner, then it would move. After that, the weight of the rock will do the rest. But to be sure we would require maybe ten or twelve sticks."

"Okay. We'll place the others more carefully. And the access?"

"It is not difficult," Bjornstrom said. "A crevice not far above the ledge where we came in is near enough to the slab for the explosive to work. But it must be done while everyone is in the shelter because the crevice is inside the arch and the man putting it there can be visible to any person on the quay or in the gallery."

"No sweat," Bolan said. "If necessary we'll create a diversion!"

14

"You know the technique," Bolan said. "For each charge you take a watch, pry out the glass and drill a small hole in it. Then break off the minute and second hands and scrape the luminous paint off the hour hand so that the naked metal is exposed."

Demonstrating with his knife blade, he continued, "Snap the glass back in place with the hole above the numeral 11 or 12 and incorporate the watchcase in a circuit including a battery and detonator. Solder the free end of your copper wire to one of the steel drawing pins and insert it through the hole. All you have to do then is push the detonator into the plastic, wind the watch and set the hour hand as far back as you need. That gives you a delay of anything from one to eleven hours."

Bjornstrom nodded. "The watch ticks away. When the hour hand touches the shank of the pin, the circuit is completed . . . and up she goes!"

They made a production line out of it. Erika removed the watch glasses and handed them to Bjornstrom, who drilled the holes. Bolan doctored the watch hands. Then, while the two men wired up each watchcase in series with a battery and detonator, she "soldered" the free end of each circuit to a pin with superglue.

Bolan had made a list, allocating where each of the thirty-six sticks of C4 should be placed—triple bundles for the elevator mechanism at the foot of the shaft and each of the three generators; doubles for the transformer and lock gates; and single sticks for the switchboard, the sluice controls and the most vulnerable installations operated from the control room.

Finally each charge was taped into a neat package with the watch on top ready for winding and setting.

The twelve packages were divided between the two neoprene sacks Bolan had salvaged from the kayak and an oiled silk pouch provided by Erika.

The Norwegian woman herself insisted that she accompany them into the secret base and help place the charges. At first Bolan objected but he was overruled by Bjornstrom.

"I shall give the orders relating to her," he said firmly. "We work together. We are a team. She is trained in this kind of operation. Besides, it is safer and more efficient and it will cut the time we have to be inside the caves by thirty percent."

This Bolan could not deny. They agreed, then, that Erika, wearing her rubber dry-suit with the oiled silk pouch strapped to her waist, would swim in via the smallest of the caves and remain in the second chamber, from which she would attend to the three generator turbines and their supply pipes plus the transformer and switchboard, which she could approach from the rear.

Wet-suited and carrying one neoprene sack each, Bolan and the Icelander would handle the rest.

Bjornstrom, because he was familiar with the local rock formations, was to place the big charge destined to block the entrance and then run through the gallery to sabotage the mine shaft.

Bolan reserved for himself the operating gear and electronics in the control room. He was also to place the vital charge that would damage the lock gates—and, if it was successful, let water into the dry-dock and flood the construction chamber.

"And the time lag?" Bjornstrom asked.

Bolan fingered his jaw. "We have to wind and set the watches before we leave," he said slowly. "Allow a half hour to swim as far as the caves and another to make it inside. Then we'll need to wait out at least three work stoppages before we get the stuff in place. They start the first shift at seven. Suppose they're ready to blow *their* first charge on the rock face around eight. Could be we won't all be clear of the place before eleven. I'd say four o'clock in the afternoon would be a good time to blow."

"Four, three, two, one, twelve, eleven..." Bjornstrom counted off the hours on his fingers. "So if we wrap up all the preparations and leave here for the caves at 6:00 A.M., we should allow a ten-hour countdown?"

Bolan nodded. "That should give us plenty of time—a big enough margin to leave the whole area before anyone starts asking awkward questions about foreigners."

"The pins are inserted between eleven and twelve on the watch faces," Erika said. "So—working backward from there—we must set the hour hands between one and two o'clock when we wind them?"

"That's my girl!" Bolan said without thinking. And intercepted a look from Erika of such frank approval that he felt embarrassed. "Just a manner of speaking," he mumbled with a smile.

She gazed straight into his eyes. "It could be a manner of action," she said. Bolan shifted uncomfortably and shot a sideways glance at Bjornstrom.

"Gunnar and I are not lovers," Erika said. "He has a wife and child in Eskifjordur, on the east coast."

Bjornstrom nodded and grinned. "We are just good friends," he agreed. "We work together."

Slightly unnerved by this Nordic frankness, Bolan sought refuge in another cliché, a military one this time, just to play safe. "I think it's time we synchronized our watches," he said gruffly.

They made the caves without incident, and Erika dived beneath the surface to swim in via the smallest opening. It was a cold morning, with mist still blanketing the cliff tops, but a bright halo glaring through the dun overcast suggested that the sun might break through later.

Bolan and the Icelander were obliged to keep a very low profile approaching the main cavern, because there were now four hitmen posted on the spur, two of them continually scanning the openings and the cliff face above. Finally, taking advantage of the fact that the mist lay thickest on the surface of the fjord, they floated facedown and allowed themselves to be carried through by the incoming tide.

After that it was a matter of waiting, half submerged, under the arch until the first whistle blew. Once the work force had disappeared, they hauled themselves up onto the dock and made for the spiral stairway that led to the gallery and control room.

From the top of the stairs, Bolan looked through to the smaller chamber and saw Erika, shining in her black frogman gear, emerge from the water by the rowboat and hurry up the slipway. She turned, saw him and gave a quick thumbs-up before vanishing through the opening that gave onto the powerhouse cave and the generators.

Bolan and his companion checked out the routes they would have to take to their separate targets and then returned to the empty control room.

Soon after the workers returned to the chamber, whistles blew again in the cavern outside.

Hastily they shuffled themselves out of sight beneath the UHF radio bench. "Straight down to the end of the gallery

and up onto your rock site once they make the shelter,''
Bolan whispered.

They heard voices and the clang of feet on the iron stairs.
A silence. Then, over the loudspeakers in Russian, came,
''What the hell have you been doing? Hurry, you fool! No,
it's too late ! Forget the shelter—you'll have to take cover in
the control room.''

Bolan and Bjornstrom froze. They wouldn't be able to
place any charges during this stoppage! Heavy footsteps
thumped along the gallery. A man hurried into the control
room, panting. It was the guard who had been on the far
side of the cavern. His boots gleamed six inches from Bolan's head.

Two muffled explosions—heavier than any they had
heard before—shook the floor and rocked the bench above
them. Somewhere above the transmitter chassis, glass chattered momentarily. They held their breath. A third report,
and then the whistles again.

A cigarette butt dropped to the floor beside the bench and
a heel swiveled to grind it out. The acrid odor of cheap to-
bacco and wet ash blew in under the bench.

Bjornstrom sneezed.

There was a startled exclamation as the guard bent down.
Gray eyes stared unbelievingly at the two saboteurs. Hands
scrabbled for the pistol grip of the Skorpion.

Bolan reached out and grabbed the guard's ears, savagely jerking the man's head forward. At the same time
Bjornstrom rolled out from beneath the bench, seized the
boots and swept the Russian's feet from under him. The
guard crashed facedown to the floor. The noise was lost in
the sounds of workers returning to the work project. Bolan
and the Icelander were on top of the guy before he could
even cry out. Bjornstrom pulled off his helmet and jammed
it back to front over the man's head, masking his face. At
the same time Bolan's hand clamped over his mouth and

jaw. Desperately trying to drag in air, the guard succeeded only in plastering the suffocating rubber device more firmly against his nostrils.

He was a strong man, threshing wildly from side to side on the concrete, but now Bjornstrom was kneeling on his biceps, pinning both arms, and the Executioner had thrown the whole weight of his body across the legs, heaving up and down as the knees jerked spasmodically.

Bjornstrom's hands went around the guard's throat and squeezed. The muffled cries behind the neoprene mask lapsed into a gurgle that rapidly diminished.

It took less than a minute for oxygen deprivation to sap the energy from the strangled man's fluttering muscles, another fifty-five seconds before the frantic thumping of the heart was stilled.

They rolled the body under the bench. Bolan rubbed a forearm across his brow. He was sweating. "I hated to do that," he whispered, "but sometimes there's no other way."

It was almost an hour before the whistles sounded again.

Bolan in the meantime had stripped jackboots, combat fatigues and miner's helmet from the dead man, and pulled them on over his wet suit. Fortunately the guard had been as tall as the Executioner and much wider.

For those fifty-plus dry-throated and agonizing minutes, Bolan patrolled the gallery. As much of the time as he believably could, he spent near the control room, out of sight of the two overseers in their steel-shuttered cubbyhole.

When he did circle over the lock gates and make the far side, he kept his head turned away and down as if he was paying particular attention to the quays below. But his hands were clammy around the butt and barrel of the Skorpion machine pistol, the hairs pricked on the nape of his neck each time he passed near the shutters, and it was with a vast sigh of relief that he finally heard the signal to take shelter.

Heading for the entrance before the others came up the stairway, he ducked behind the stack of oil drums at the last minute and allowed them all to pass.

As soon as the dock was deserted, Bjornstrom was out of the control room and speeding along the gallery. He had vaulted the rail and clambered up along the weathered outcrops that were tiered above the opening to the cave before the first detonation.

Bolan was back in the control room, taping primed sticks of plastic among the operating levers, beneath the bench, in back of the computer console.

Screwing an inspection cover back in place, he saw through a window that Bjornstrom was spread-eagled over a slab of granite immediately above the channel leading in from the fjord. It was late morning now, and the sun must have dissipated the mist, because there was a bright glare on the water that reflected chevrons and crescents of light across the vaulted roof of the cavern.

From where he was, Bolan was unable to see clearly just what the Icelander was doing. He could not distinguish the slab of granite that had jammed across a gap and prevented the cliff from tumbling into the fjord—the quartzite, shining with damp and alive with reflections, looked as solid as any mountain he had seen. Perhaps the fractures were more easily identifiable from outside.

Cautiously he emerged from the control room—now the final charge for the dock gates.

Blast assaulted his eardrums. A puff of warm air followed the explosion, the loudest yet, and a shower of rock fragments clattered among the ironwork of the scaffolding. Splashes pitted the surface of the water below. Several jagged pieces of quartzite whistled past the Executioner like shrapnel.

He dodged momentarily behind the oil drums.

Bjornstrom appeared to be hard at work still. His left arm vanished into a crevice.

There was another, small explosion...and, almost at once, the whistles blew.

Bolan swore beneath his breath. The all-clear had taken him completely by surprise—there had been far less time lag than usual. His fellow saboteur was crucified on the rock face. He couldn't possibly climb down and make the shelter of the drums before the Russians emerged from their refuge; not could it be safe to retreat the way they had come in the first time—there were guards on the spur, and in any case he would be spotted from inside before he could edge out of sight around the corner of the arch.

Desperately Bolan glanced over his shoulder. He heard the sound of footsteps and voices coming from outside the doorway leading to the shelter. In a moment the workers would be flooding out and onto the stairway. In the few seconds that remained there was only one thing for the Icelander to do—and Bolan dared not raise his voice to suggest it.

But Bjornstrom realized the plight he was in. With a quick turn of the head to check that Bolan was still watching, he raised a hand in salute, let go his hold on the rock and dropped twenty feet into the water.

There was enough height to allow him to jackknife before he went in. His outstretched fingertips arrowed through the surface, and he disappeared with scarcely a splash to mark his passage. By the time the Russians reached the gallery, his dark shape was lost among fronds of seaweed in the shadowy depths of the entrance, and the few ripples he had made on his way out were swallowed up in the interplay of light below the arch as the tide sucked and lapped its way into the basin.

For the second time Bolan sighed with relief. He lowered his head and shoulders behind the drums, waiting for work to resume before he continued his perilous impersonation.

Had Bjornstrom succeeded in placing his charge? Was the plastic in the best position for toppling the granite? There was no way he could tell. Bjornstrom would either have to swim back to the rocks where the raft was hidden or attempt to join Erika in the smaller cavern.

One thing was certain—the man who worked for the Norwegian secret service would not be able to sabotage the mine shaft and the elevator now.

So how best to use his own remaining charge? Bolan weighed the pros and cons. The lock gates or the elevator shaft?

He decided on the shaft. The odds against a successful attack on the gates increased with every second—the dead guard could be missed at any time and that would put the entire place on general alert; to cripple the gates, it would be necessary to lodge the plastic explosive among the hinge mechanism or actually between them, and in either case that involved an underwater operation; if he was to dive, Bolan must discard the guard's uniform and that would hasten the chances of discovery; finally it was possible that the work force might break for lunch soon, and that meant no more whistle-stops.

This time he did not have to wait so long.

Checking that the two overseers in the hutch were still facing the dry-dock, he followed the last of the Russians through the doorway... but instead of heading for the shelter, he dropped to his hands and knees, crawled past the steel shutters below window level and then ran for the warren of passageways beyond.

He chose the one leading directly away from the basin. It rose steeply upward and ended in a circular chamber from which several tunnels led off. The highest and widest—

which had evidently been used for the transportation of plant from the elevator to the submarine pens—was roughly hewed from the rock, supported every few yards by pit props and cross beams and dimly lit by low-power electric lamps. A current of cool air blew along it, which the warrior guessed must originate at the foot of the shaft.

He hurried along the tunnel, turned a corner and was faced with a T-junction. Licking one finger and holding it up, he found that the draft came from the left. As he set off in that direction there was a dull concussion somewhere behind him, and his ears cracked momentarily as the pressure in the passageway altered.

A few yards farther on a second blast, a series of small detonations dimmed the lights.

Bolan figured he must still be almost two hundred yards from the mine shaft. Before he was halfway there, he heard the faint shrilling of whistles. He would have to pull out all the stops if he was to plant his explosive before the risk of encountering one of the guards became unacceptable.

The elevator cage was at the pithead—a diminutive plug blocking the light at the top of a vertical shaft stretching far up into the dark. The winching equipment, the huge counterweight and the arrangement of wire hawsers in the circular rock well at the bottom of the shaft could have been designed to operate a passenger elevator in some prehistoric subway station, Bolan thought with a smile.

But there was nothing prehistoric about the footsteps he could hear advancing far away in the maze of passageways near the dock basin.

Reaching into the neoprene pouch, he drew out the remaining two-stick delayed-action charge, checked that the watch was ticking and correctly set, and jumped lightly down into the elevator well.

Ten seconds later, he pulled his hand back from the underside of an inspection hatch with an exclamation of astonishment.

There was already a charge in place there—time-fused, neatly bundled and taped securely in place.

Before he had time to think, a voice said softly behind him, "There is a saying in your country, I believe, that great minds think alike. It is good to find that this is true!"

Bolan whirled. He was facing Bjornstrom, the wet suit still damply gleaming in the wan underground lighting. "How the hell did you get here?" Bolan demanded in a whisper.

"Swam around into the smallest cave and found a tunnel that led here directly. Very convenient—and it does not seem to be patrolled."

"Great." Bolan glanced at the shaft. "Might as well leave my charge here, too. We won't have time to go back to the dock."

"There is a fissure that runs halfway around the shaft," the Icelander said. "If you push it in there, as well as destroying the mechanism we might also bring down some rock and wreck the shaft."

"Better still." Bolan was shoving the package as far into the crevice as it would go when they heard shouting in the distance followed by the insistent clamor of an alarm bell.

"I think they have found the dead guard," Bjornstrom said.

15

Shouted commands and the clump of booted feet drowned the sounds of the sea throughout the underground complex. The shrilling alarm bell punctuated orders rasping through speakers fixed to the rock walls at the corner of every passageway.

"We are lucky," Bolan panted, "that they didn't monitor the whole place with closed-circuit TV."

Bjornstrom had led him to an unlit opening on the far side of the elevator well, and they were hotfooting it back to the smallest cave.

"Whatever happens," Bolan insisted, "they mustn't know we penetrated as far as the mine shaft. They'll know we made the control room—that's where they found the body. But I want them to think that was as far as we got; I want them to believe we only just made it to the cavern, that we were on our way *in* when the guy surprised us."

"How can we do that?" Bjornstrom demanded. The route was far shorter than the one Bolan had taken, and they were already approaching the cave.

Bolan stared across at the water swilling around the slipway. "We must get back to that stack of oil drums," he said, "and let them find us hiding there. Then we split. They have to think they surprised us at the start of a recon trip—not the end of a sabotage mission. Otherwise they'll start poking around here and there to see where we went. And if they discover one of the charges..." He shrugged, leaving the sentence unfinished.

"Is there any way we could use the uniform you're wearing? Could we maybe fool them—" Bjornstrom began.

"Uh-uh." Bolan cut him short. "Don't forget we stripped the dead guard, so they'll be looking for someone wearing his uniform...." Bolan paused. He was gazing pensively at the slipway. "Still...it's an idea...maybe we can make use of it in a different way."

Hastily he pulled off the boots and coverall and stuffed them into the neoprene sack that now contained nothing but his AutoMag and a spare clip of ammunition. He lowered himself into the water. The numbing shock of the sudden immersion was like a blow in the solar plexus, but he mastered the cramp and swam fast across to the slipway.

Clinging to the rowboat moored beside it, he unzipped the sack one-handed and laid boots and coverall along the duckboards. Finally he removed the miner's helmet he was still wearing and placed it above the gray fatigues. In poor light, for a few seconds, it was just possible that a distant watcher might mistakenly believe a man was lying prone below the gunwales.

Very carefully, Bolan unhitched the painter, submerged himself and swam slowly out toward the center of the cavern, pushing the boat before him.

When it was framed in the rock arch between the two chambers, he gave it a final shove and then backed off. The tide was ebbing, and a slight current receding toward the fjord carried the craft in the direction of the smallest cave entrance.

As he had hoped, the movement of the rowboat, as it floated through the shaft of light streaming in from the main cavern, was seen by someone. There was an excited shout, followed by two more. The ringing of alarm bells stopped, and an amplified voice rapped orders through the speaker system.

Gunfire ripped out, reverberating around the linked caves like thunder in the mountains. Pale marks peppered the dark planking of the rowboat as heavy slugs splintered the wood. The vessel lurched slightly under the impacts and spun slowly around.

Boots clattered on the iron stairway. A muttered conference distorted a dozen times by the sea-wet rock faces echoed sibilantly overhead. Then at last there was silence— an eerie quiet broken only by the lap and suck of the water; a stillness continually contradicted by the ceaseless interplay of light reflected onto the crystalline roof by the movement of the tide.

The Russians were clearly planning some surprise move— based on the belief that they had eliminated an intruder in the boat.

It was the diversion Bolan had hoped for. He motioned to the Icelander, and together they dived underwater and swam through the arch into the submarine pens beneath the gallery. Bolan surfaced by the dockside.

Abruptly, from behind him, he heard a rush of footsteps along the quay they had just left in the smaller basin. The pursuers had raced through the network of passages in the hope of catching unawares whoever was connected with the boat. By now they would be wise to the fact that the craft itself was no more than a decoy.

More commands rapped out in Russian over the speakers. Followed by Bjornstrom, the Executioner hoisted himself onto the concrete dockside and together they sped silently up the spiral ladder to the stack of drums.

There were men on the far side of the gallery, but they were all concentrating their attention on the far cave. By the drums, Bolan made a brusque movement to catch their eyes. Four out of the half dozen swung around at once.

Four SMGs roared a hymn of hate through the caves. Rock chips showered Bolan's side of the gallery; oil gushed from punctured drums.

The two saboteurs had ripped open their neoprene sacks in readiness. Facedown below the gallery railing, they returned fire. Bjornstrom's compact sixteen-inch Ingram chattered out a stream of lethal skull busters, and the Executioner's AutoMag punctuated the death stream with individual shots that bellowed beneath the cavern roof.

Two of the Russians fell forward over the rail and dropped into the dock basin, where they floated lifelessly, trailing clouds of crimson in the dark water. A third was hurled back against the wall, his arm shattering on impact.

"Okay," Bolan yelled. "Now! We've been surprised—and beaten back—on the way in. Let's go!"

Vaulting over the rail, they dived into the basin and swam frantically underwater for the cave entrance. With luck the guards outside on the spur wouldn't know what the hell was going on; with luck they wouldn't be in direct contact with the speaker system; with luck Bolan and his companion could stay submerged long enough, once they were through the arch, to escape their attention.

With luck.

It was when he surfaced to catch his breath beneath the arch that Bolan heard, over the sporadic shots still being fired after them, the shouts from the inner cave that were followed by a woman's scream.

With a sick feeling in the pit of his stomach, he realized that, in decoying the main body of the Russians into the second chamber, he had unwittingly delivered Erika Axelsson into the hands of the enemy.

16

"She is safe for another three hours," Bjornstrom said. "She does after all have the pill with her."

"The pill?" Bolan sounded incredulous. "You don't mean . . . ? Not the cyanide pill?"

"No, no. Nothing so . . . final. A kind of a sleeping pill, except that it acts instantly. It's a variety of chloral hydrate, your old-fashioned Mickey Finn, without the hangover. They can do nothing to her, she will hear nothing and feel nothing, until the effect wears off."

"You said three hours?"

"Four from the time she bit down on it. They give them to us in our service—it leaves time to attempt a rescue before they start to torture a prisoner. There is no point administering electric shocks to someone who is—how do you say?—out for the count."

"But three hours from now?" It was not quite midday. Bolan and the Icelander were holding a conference of war over glasses of Brennevin and weak local beer in a tavern on the outskirts of Pvera, on the far side of the fjord from the Russian concession. "That means we have to bust into the place and get her out by three o'clock this afternoon, right?"

"I think so," Bjornstrom said soberly.

The mission is more important than individual members of the team—this was the hard lesson Bolan had to learn in Nam, in the Mafia wars and during his subsequent antiterrorist campaign. It was a truism for military men the world over. But that didn't mean you wouldn't do your damndest to get back a fellow fighter in enemy hands... *before* that operation could compromise the mission.

In any case this one was a self-imposed mission. Even if the time element had not been in favor of a quick rescue attempt, no alternative entered the Executioner's mind; no other line of action would have occurred to him. Erika was a comrade in arms. She had been captured; she must be released. As quickly as possible. It was that simple.

"How are we going to do it?" Bjornstrom said.

Before Bolan could reply, a tall, elderly man with white hair and thick-lensed glasses detached himself from a group of young people and advanced on Bolan. He held out his hand. "Good to see you again," he said affably. "I guess you made your run down to Jokulsa after all?"

Astonished, Bolan automatically took the hand, thinking; who the hell is this? The face was vaguely familiar but he could not place it; neither the voice nor the presence stirred any connection in his memory.

"The plane," the old-timer reminded him. "The flight from Copenhagen."

Of course. Bolan remembered. So much had happened since then that he had completely forgotten the conversation with the passenger sitting next to him on the Icelandair 727.

But then an ugly doubt surfaced in his mind. *Could this man be the contact who had tipped off the Russians that a guy known as the Executioner was on his way?*

Uh-uh. Looking beyond the white-haired guy to the group he had left, he recalled the rest of it. They were college kids. Boys and girls. He remembered them leaving Keflavik field while he was checking out his freight, bound for the capital on a bus. Geology students, and the old man was their professor.

"Yeah," he said in answer to the professor's question. "I finally made it. A fairly...eventful...journey. I hope your own expedition has been successful," he added politely, wondering how he could get rid of the elderly academic.

"Not as interesting as yours, I'm afraid," the professor replied. "We can't all cross the lava fields in kayaks! However, this afternoon should prove stimulating. The Russians leasing the promontory on the far side of the fjord have kindly offered to show us over the trial bores they are sinking among the igneous intrusions."

Bolan caught his breath. "This...afternoon?" he echoed.

"That's right. It seems there are uncharacteristic pegmatites among the amphiboles and plagioclase zones they encountered in their search for tin lodes. They promise to let us explore the upper galleries."

"What time?" Bolan asked urgently. "What time this afternoon?"

The professor raised his brows, surprised at the Executioner's tone of voice. "Three-thirty, actually," he said. "We are required to make a punctual appearance at the main gate. It seems they are rather hot on security, and we have to be escorted to the pithead."

Bolan excused himself as quickly as he could and rejoined Bjornstrom. This time he was really shaken. Not only was Erika in the hands of the Russians, a party of college kids were being shown over the upper section of the mine workings at the very time the charges they had so carefully timed were due to explode.

Somehow, within the next three hours, they had to spirit the girl away and save the students from almost certain death.

"We must go back in and alter the timing," Bjornstrom said. "Push the hour hands right back again so the charges will not go off until late this evening."

"No way." Bolan shook his head. "There are twelve of them. Each one has to be located, unwrapped, retimed, taped back in position and then concealed again. That takes a lot more time than just shoving a prepared package in among the machinery. We'd never make it; there wouldn't be enough work stoppages for one thing."

"But if we concentrated first on those nearest the shaft, the charges putting the kids in most danger?"

"We might not be able to concentrate on any. For all we know they may not be blasting at all this afternoon. Especially if they have a conducted tour planned."

"Then...?" The Icelander looked crushed.

"We'll play it another way. We'll go back in all right. But we won't touch the charges; we won't go near them. We'll simply use the caves as an entry to the surface workings."

"You're crazy."

"Like a fox, Gunnar. We'll have to play it damned close to the chest, but it can be done. We have three objectives—destroy the base, rescue Erika and save the kids, right?"

"So?"

"So what's wrong with making all three in a single operation?"

"I cannot see how it is possible," Bjornstrom said.

"I'll tell you," Bolan told him. "If we leave the charges the way they are we achieve objective number one, anyway. So all that remains is to get Erika out—and stop the students going in."

"This is where *I* come in, Bolan. How the hell—?"

"Listen. All we have to do is get to that elevator. If they are still blasting, we do it while they're in the shelter; if not, we'll blast our own way in there. With lead. Once we make the cage, we take it to the top and come out shooting. We locate Erika...and then we stage the biggest, boldest, most ear-shattering battle the Russians have seen for a long time."

"After we have Erika? Why don't we just get out? If that is not just a pipe dream anyway?"

"You don't understand. The Sovs are obviously asking these Danish kids and their instructor around as a PR exercise. They won't allow them anyplace near the submarine pens. But it consolidates their position, strengthens their cover if independent witnesses actually see them doing their mining number. If we raise enough hell, on the other hand, the Russians themselves will find some way to stop the kids coming in. The last thing they'll want is an audience if the place is humming with live rounds from Ingrams and Kalashnikovs!"

Bjornstrom passed a hand over his face. "Well," he said, "it might work." He sighed heavily. "I suppose."

"It's got to work," the Executioner said.

BY THE TIME the security guards got Erika Axelsson to the pithead she was already under the effects of the pill. They took her to a room behind the chief overseer's office, ripped the latex dry-suit down around her ankles, hosed her with icy water and beat her naked body with rubber hoses. But though her breasts, belly and buttocks turned black and blue she showed no reaction.

She remained comatose when a 12-volt electric current from a hand-cranked generator was jolted through her body, and there was no muscular reflex when one of the guards stubbed out a cigarette on her wrist.

"It's no good," the station doctor told them. "It's pointless applying stimuli, useless to ask questions. She is genuinely, deeply unconscious."

The KGB colonel in charge of security was furious. "How long," he raged, "before the bitch will be in a fit state to be questioned?"

The doctor shrugged. "Difficult to say. Depends on the exact composition of the drug—it's some kind of chloral hydrate compound. And of course on the amount in the pill. Clearly it will be fairly efficient, or she would not have been provided with it. I say several hours at least.''

COLONEL DMITRI ALEKSANDREVITCH ANTONIN became increasingly frustrated as he pondered his present circumstances.

He had once been liaison between the KGB and GRU military intelligence. In that function he had been assistant to the infamous Major General Greb Strakhov of the KGB hierarchy. The Iceland posting was a demotion. It had come as a result of Antonin's failure to organize a worldwide Mafia confederation that was to have been backed with KGB money.

The man responsible for that failure, for provoking such internecine strife among the various Mob families that the idea had to be abandoned as impracticable, was Mack Bolan.

Not Colonel Antonin's favorite character, now or at any time.

It was bad enough that they had crossed swords not just that once but many times . . . and the American had always come out on top. The worst thing of all was that Bolan should have turned up right here, in Iceland, at the exact time Antonin hoped for a spectacular success that would reestablish him in the eyes of Moscow.

How had the bastard known?

The commercial attaché from the Soviet embassy who happened to recognize him on the plane from Denmark had done well to signal Antonin at once. Yet the capitalist lackey had four times outwitted KGB assassins before he even arrived at the sinkhole in the glacier.

Since then there had been nothing but disasters.

The crews of two outposts on the river annihilated, a helicopter and its occupants destroyed at the pumping station near Grimsstadir by Bolan and some as yet unidentified accomplice, five men and a raft vanished without trace at the Fjallagfoss, a vehicle and another five operatives lost on the road near the lakehead. And Bolan, unscathed, was still advancing as remorselessly as the tides that Antonin had made part of his own blueprint for success.

The man was not human.

Worst of all, he had somehow wormed out the secret of the caves and attempted—for once, thank God, unsuccessfully—to penetrate the base.

Now this unknown woman associated with the foreign terrorist and his companion had materialized. And even here Antonin was temporarily blocked from wringing the information he craved out of her.

No matter. She was in his hands. He had learned how to play the waiting game. The moment she regained consciousness she would be made to talk. It would be a pleasure to assist at the ceremony. And then he would know precisely how much the mercenary, Bolan, had discovered . . . and how best to rid himself of the implacable Westerner who had so often—too often—proved a stumbling block in Antonin's own carefully prepared plans.

It never occurred to the wily Russian that the whole series of setbacks might derive from a simple coincidence. That if the attaché had not been so overzealous—Bolan might simply have continued his vacation and not noticed anything amiss. If the Executioner had not been pursued so doggedly by KGB killers, which made him so determined to find out what was going on, he might have shrugged the whole thing off as none of his business. But those who make a profession out of deceit are incapable of comprehending the truth themselves.

Antonin stalked across to the video display terminal. A naval enlisted man, cleared for top-secret work, sat at the VDT console. On the dark green fluorescent screen, multiple blips located units of the NATO and Soviet fleets operating in the area.

Russia's northern fleet, largest and strongest of four, was based well over one thousand miles away at Murmansk and other ports on the Kola Peninsula. Yet the Soviet blips outnumbered the NATO units by more than ten to one.

There were eighty surface-combat vessels in the fleet, which included nine guided-missile cruisers, seven missile destroyers, two carriers and more than one hundred submarines. Most of them were steaming to a rendezvous sixty miles north of the Arctic Circle for an exercise designed to test their maneuverability in time of emergency—and, incidentally, to probe NATO reaction to large-scale fleet maneuvers.

Most of them... except the submarines.

The naval authorities had considered it wasteful to employ more than half a dozen nuclear craft when soon enough the new SSKs to be clandestinely based on Iceland would so radically change the pattern of naval operations in the region.

Antonin turned to a wall hanger and pulled down a large-scale polar map of the North Atlantic, a projection that emphasized the too-often-ignored proximity of the Soviet Union and the United States across the ice cap.

And the vital strategic importance of Iceland in that context.

Anchored like a monumental aircraft carrier between Greenland and Norway, the country effectively controlled all three of the sea passages through which the Russians could move their fleet into offensive positions that would be menacing to the NATO forces—the gaps between Iceland and Greenland, Iceland and the Faroe Islands and between the Faroes and Scotland.

How much easier it would be to plan such movements when the SSK hunter-killer minisubs, themselves secretly operating from the bowels of an Icelandic glacier, could monitor and, if necessary, influence the concentrations of enemy shipping that blocked any Soviet advance!

How agreeable to reflect that responsibility for the existence of a base actually within the NATO bastion would largely be his!

Antonin saw himself at a Kremlin ceremony, the Order of Lenin being pinned to his chest. He saw himself in a VIP office with a carpeted floor at 2 Dzerzhinsky Square, the KGB headquarters in Moscow; in his own imported automobile; at a country dacha with servants.

He saw himself in total charge of all the KGB directorates, planning secret operations worldwide.

The Soviet admiral in overall charge of the real-life submarine pen project on which Antonin's hopes were founded had come into the room.

He was staring at the VDT screen, a replica of the one that would shortly become operative in the control room of the cavern more than two hundred feet below them.

"Much NATO activity?" he asked the navy man at the console.

"Very little, Comrade Admiral," the man replied. "Just the flotilla engaged on this so-called goodwill mission." He pointed to a small cluster of blips at the left of the screen.

"There will be British submarines skulking around on the seabed someplace on the fringe of the exercise area," the admiral growled, "spying on our fleet and feeding the information into their damned computers in the hope of a printout that will allow them to extrapolate what we would do in any given situation."

He turned to Antonin. "I shall call up the Ilyushins to make sure that we have eyes and ears underwater; we shall beat them at their own game."

The Ilyushins—converted long-range transport planes— sowed undersea sensors copied from captured American

SOSUS detectors that could chart the course of a submarine wherever it went. The latest models were so sophisticated that they could identify individual submarines from the noise of their engine print.

"It will not be long, Comrade Admiral," Antonin said, "before such intricacies will become redundant. The short-range recon hunter-killers deployed from this base will provide quicker, better, more accurate information than any computed—"

"If the base is ever finished," the admiral interrupted tartly. "We are already weeks behind schedule. It should have been in operation well before the long-night season. And provided its existence has not been splashed over every newspaper in Northern Europe."

He looked coldly at Antonin. Neither the KGB nor the GRU were popular with the Soviet armed forces. "Your much-vaunted 'security' has not proved very secure, Comrade Colonel, has it? Our pipelines uncovered, our site penetrated, our outposts destroyed. Your professional enforcers outwitted at every turn by a single amateur guerrilla. A man still at liberty moreover. And even the guards charged with the security of our fjord entries prove incapable of resisting this terrorist. It would seem that they themselves require guarding," the admiral said sarcastically. "You have in fact already lost three of them if I am not mistaken?"

Antonin's face was suffused with rage. A vein in his temple twitched uncontrollably. He had forgotten to include the men missing from the spur in his catalog of Bolan attacks. "By nightfall the man will be in our hands and the affair terminated," he said in a choked voice.

He strode to his desk, snatched up the interphone and savagely punched buttons on the handset.

"Rodsky?" he snapped. "Prepare the woman for sharpened interrogation at once. I know she is not conscious, you dolt. Prepare her nevertheless. The interrogation is to commence as soon as she shows signs of consciousness."

17

For Mack Bolan and his Icelandic ally the most difficult part of the operation was getting back into the caves.

The sun, low in the sky but fiercely bright, flashed reflections from the binoculars wielded by four guards deployed around the spur. Two hundred feet higher, security men silhouetted against the skyline constantly scanned the fjord. And within the connecting caverns it was certain that special orders would have been given in case the impudent intruders of the morning were rash enough to try a second time.

The impudent intruders left Pvera in a beat-up Citroën that Bjornstrom had somehow acquired and raced across the bridge at the head of the fjord to take the highway leading to Akureyri. Two miles farther on, Bjornstrom swung right onto a dirt road that looped up toward the Russian concession.

While the mine workings and the wall barring the entrance were still hidden on the far side of a swell in the landscape, he turned off the road and steered between scattered boulders across a depression that ended in a steep-sided valley slanting down to the water.

Once out of sight of the road, he cut the engine and coasted. The noisy clatter of the air-cooled twin-cylinder engine died away, and they bumped across a slope of coarse moorland grass to halt in the shelter of a granite outcrop.

Below them the valley plunged toward a cascade that foamed into a creek leading off the fjord. And there, shielded by a wilderness of tumbled rocks, their Hypalon raft was concealed.

They clambered down and retrieved their wet suits from beneath the seats of the raft.

The one thing in their favor, the only factor that gave them a chance to make the caves unseen, was the fact that the concession was on the western side of the fjord.

Because of this, a combination of low afternoon sun and high cliffs threw a shadow across the water.

"Even so," Bolan said, "we shall have to make the whole distance underwater, with snorkels for both of us all the way."

"The bottom of the fjord is black basalt and marine vegetation grows below the cliffs," Bjornstrom pointed out. "There's no pale seabed sand for us to show up against. You don't think—?"

"No way," Bolan insisted. "It's okay for minisubs—they will be at some depth; no danger of them leaving a telltale wash. But even if we are invisible below, the moment we broke surface to gulp in a breath of air we'd risk making enough of a commotion to draw the attention of the goons on that spur. Or one of the guards above. They might take it for a fish after a fly the first time, but not the next. Anyway, they'd probably loose off a burst just in case."

"Whatever you say," Bjornstrom agreed.

He sloshed water around inside the eyepiece of his mask, pulled it down over his face and took the hard rubber breathing bit between his teeth. Followed by the Executioner, he submerged and swam slowly out of the creek into the fjord.

Even with the snorkels they had to take it slowly. In the circumstances it was difficult to remain underwater for much more than a minute. And each time the head of a breathing tube with its caged ball valve periscoped above the surface there was a chance it might leave enough wake to alert a watcher.

Fortunately the tide was now rising. The inward flow of seawater meeting the current of the Jokulsa a Fjollum created ripples on the shadowed side of the fjord and a constant, shifting glimmer of sunlight beyond.

Each of them was hampered in his movements, Bolan with the waterproof Heckler & Koch G-11 strapped across his chest, the Icelander by the neoprene sack protecting his Ingram and two handguns. In addition, each stroke had to be made cautiously, the breath drawn evenly and slowly when the U-shaped tube broke surface and the ball float dropped to let in air.

It was almost two o'clock before they arrived at the mouth of the smallest cave.

They surfaced still in the shelter of the low rock arch and trod water, staring into the lit interior of the small cavern.

The rowboat had been pulled out of the water and up to the top of the slipway. The only other difference from their previous visit was that now the entry to the generator cave and each of the passageways branching off the quay framed a guard with a Skorpion machine pistol.

Over the hum of turbines the two men could hear the familiar sounds of drills, compressors and concrete mixers. Work was evidently continuing on the rock faces around and behind the caisson.

From time to time an overseer shouted an order, but the noise was mainly mechanical. The guards did not patrol. They remained motionless at their posts.

Clinging to the rough walls just outside the pool of light, the roof of the arch low above their heads with the rising tide, the two freedom fighters waited for the whistle to blow. Would the KGB hardmen barring their way go to the shelter with the others?

No whistle.

Thirty-five minutes passed.

Bolan and his companion were numbed with cold, their circulation sluggish through lack of activity. Finally the Executioner touched Bjornstrom on the arm and jerked his head toward the entrance.

They submerged again, swam out below the cliff and dived in once more via the center arch, surfacing where the channel curved just before it joined the main cavern.

The scene was familiar—workers swarming over the scaffolding above the construction site, overseers stalking this way and that, electric cables and compressor tubes snaking over the quays beneath the blazing arcs.

Six guards stood on the gallery.

Three men were posted on the far side, staring down into the water. One was in front of the control room, another by the stack of drums and the last outside the hut from which the blasting was controlled. The air was heavy with the stink of fuel oil spilled from drums punctured during the morning shoot-out.

And still no whistle blew.

Bolan floated to the far side of the tunnel, from where he could steal an upward glance at the hut.

Behind the steel shutters the brightly lit shack was empty.

He had been right—no blasting this afternoon.

He flicked a glance at his watch. The luminous digits told him that it was a quarter to three.

Fifteen minutes before Erika came to, helpless in the hands of KGB torturers. Bolan had no illusions about what would happen to her if he didn't get there first.

"Attention! Attention!" The amplified voice rasped around the caverns from the PA speakers in Russian. "Operation Crystal. Overseers and work force are to return to surface immediately for briefing on simulated mining activity in upper gallery. Brosolov, Rott, Shepelev, Brodsky,

Korsun and Radin are to remain below on constant patrol. The remainder of the guards to the pithead."

"Wising them up on the routine to be followed when the prof and his college kids arrive," Bolan whispered. "This is our only chance."

With no more than six guards, and those continually on the move, he was confident that he could blast his way through to the shaft. Yeah, Brosolov, Rott and their fellow thugs were going to be real sorry they didn't make the surface with the others.

"We'll wait to see how they deploy," he murmured to Bjornstrom. "And take three each once they separate."

"We have very little time left." Bjornstrom's face was creased with anxiety. "Erika—"

"I know. But a slug doesn't waste time making it from muzzle to target," the warrior reassured him grimly.

The sounds of work ceased. Compressors fell silent. When the workers and overseers had trooped away to the elevator, the guards left behind started to patrol. Two pairs of boots clattered down the iron stairway. One man remained up on the far side of the gallery. Bolan reckoned that the others must still be around the smaller basin in the other cave.

Beckoning Bjornstrom to follow, the Executioner swam quickly through into the dock. Pulling himself up onto the quayside, he shook drops of water from the streamlined casing of the G-11 and sprinted for the lock gates at the inner end of the basin. The Icelander sidled through the arch separating the two chambers.

Bolan had been seen. There was a shout from the gallery. He vaulted the nearest of the gates and crouched on the catwalk, crossing it as a fusillade ripped out from the gallery and splatted against the steel casing.

Bolan planted his elbows on the flange that topped the gate, then swung up the caseless assault rifle, squinted through the optical handle sight and triggered a 3-round 90-millisecond burst at the KGB goon before he could fire again.

The three reports coughed out as a single snarling bark.

A trio of pint-size death bringers cored through both of the Russian's hands, jerking the Skorpion upward before they slammed on to pierce his heart. Death tightened his trigger finger in the instant that he was hurled backward against the rock wall by the manic force of the tiny slugs, spraying the contents of the machine pistol's magazine roofward to shatter one of the batteries of arc lights.

Reflectors, fragments of aluminum casing and broken glass showered down into the water. At the same time Bolan heard two much heavier splashes from the direction of the inner basin. Bjornstrom, now using a MAC suppressor on his Ingram, must have profited from the silencing facility to down two more of the opposition.

Three down, three up.

The pair who had thumped down the spiral stairway must by now have located Bolan—the short burst from his G-11 had echoed from wall to wall of the cavern complex but there could be no doubt where it originated.

The warrior decided to draw their fire. He would give them something to shoot at. He raced to the far end of the catwalk and leaped up among the scaffolding above the caisson.

Slugs screamed off the metal stays and smashed into the rock beyond as first one Skorpion, then another, blazed out murderous volleys.

Bolan was ready. The muzzle-flashes had flickered from a patch of shadow beneath the arch separating the two basins. He fired from the hip, stitching together the two pools of light with hellfire thread.

The figure-eight death stream seamed the two guards.

They caromed off the wall and slumped sideways, one into each pool of light. The far one, his chest burst open like a sausage under a grill, fell near the edge of the walkway linking the two caves. Blood bubbled out from beneath him, flowed over the stone lip and clouded the water below.

The second man, illuminated by the light in the main cavern, was still moving. An arm, perforated by splinters of bone, twitched. Splayed fingers reached for the fallen Skorpion.

The face, mouth open and eyes crazed, filled the eyepiece of Bolan's optical sight with hate. He coaxed another miniburst from the G-11 and transformed it into a gory pulp.

Where was the sixth man?

The sound of running footsteps pounded the gallery. The guy shot into view from one of the tunnels opening off the cave and dashed for the one that led to the shelter and the steel-shuttered hut from which the blasting was directed.

Bolan's field of fire was obscured by the scaffolding. From where he was he didn't have a hope of getting back up to the gallery in time.

"Gunnar!" he yelled. "The radio, the phone! Stop him before he—"

The words died in his mouth. Bjornstrom had appeared in another of the rock openings. He took in the scene at a glance, raced halfway along the gallery...and stopped dead.

Through the slats of the shutters, he could see the guard grabbing a handset hooked to an instrument fixed on the wall. Whatever happened, the Norwegian knew that the Russians on the surface must not be warned that anything was wrong below.

Without the element of surprise their plan was useless and they would be dead before they got anywhere near Erika.

Bjornstrom had one of the handguns—it was Bolan's AutoMag—in his fist. He took a snap sight and fired.

The report of the wildcat .44-caliber shell was deafening. And the force of the recoil took the Icelander off guard. He miscalculated the rise, and the slug caught the edge of a steel slat high up the window and whined off into the darkness of the roof. Glass tinkled to the floor.

The guard dropped the receiver and snatched his machine pistol from a desk beside the window. Before he raised the barrel, Bjornstrom fired again. This time his aim was better. The 240-grain hollowpoint caught the man full in the throat.

For a heart-stopping moment, as the Russian's mouth opened in astonishment, a scarlet flower bloomed horribly against the whiteness of his skin. Then he toppled to the floor spewing blood, his head almost severed from his body.

Bolan and Bjornstrom arrived at the door of the hut at the same time. The Executioner saw that the telephone handset was still swinging at the end of its lead. He picked it up and hooked it gently back on its cradle. The machine, one of the few outdated devices in the Russian base, was one of those with a hand-cranked generator, which rang a bell at the other end of the line—like an army field telephone.

"Did you get him before he turned the handle?" Bolan asked urgently.

Bjornstrom nodded.

The warrior breathed a sigh of relief. No listening gear would have been alerted on the surface.

"There's no service stairway," he said lightly. "We'll take the elevator to the top floor!"

18

The elevator cage was wide enough to take three jeeps side by side. It was closed by a hand-operated latticework grille that ran noisily on rollers.

As it rose into the darkness from the brightly lit underground chamber, Bolan could imagine the big wheel at the pithead turning. Would there be guards alerted up there on the surface, waiting to mow them down the moment they made ground level? Had any of the Russians noticed when they brought the cage creaking down five minutes ago?

The Executioner thought not.

It was no more than a hunch, but it was based on solid reasoning.

The relayed announcement had ordered the work force back to the surface for "briefing on simulated mining activity." The students were due in half an hour. It was likely, therefore, that all available personnel would be required at the briefing, to make sure they knew what they were supposed to do during the conducted tour. Also, it was unlikely during this period that anyone would return to the cavern; because of this, there was a good chance there would be nobody at the top of the shaft to check whether the elevator was up or down. Since the concession was protected on three sides by sheer cliffs, and on the fourth by a wall patrolled by armed men, there was no need to post a guard there.

But it was only a hunch. And there was a chance. In any case there was nothing else he could do. And a fighter should always be prepared to back his own hunches, right?

There were oil drums in back of the elevator cage. Replacements, maybe, for those punctured this morning, which nobody'd had time to shift? Bolan and the Icelander squatted behind them. Bjornstrom held the silenced Ingram, Bolan the G-11. Each carried one of the handguns from the neoprene pouch in waterproof shoulder rigs—Bolan this time with Big Thunder, Bjornstrom toting his Beretta.

The elevator jolted to a halt.

Light flooded through the grille. The two men crouched, weapons ready. Inside the cage, only their quiet breathing broke the silence. Outside, sunlight glinted off a baggage trolley loaded with flat pans of yellowish ore, and from corrugated iron roofing.

But there were no KGB guards waiting on the packed earth surrounding the shaft. A row of huts in front appeared to be deserted, and the cars and trucks ranged behind in a lot excavated from the hillside were all empty. Bolan's hunch had paid off—nobody had seen the elevator descend, then return.

He rose, stole quietly to the grille, held up his hand. They could hear a voice, amplified, speaking in Russian. It seemed to come from the slope of hillside below the huts.

"It is essential," the speaker emphasized, "that what you are doing appears to be a routine, something you are used to doing. Groups A and D therefore will be sinking exploratory holes farther out on the headland; Group C will list analyzed samples of the cores they have brought up; Group E will be working the upper trial gallery and Group B will remain with myself and the Comrade Admiral, supervising and acting as interpreters."

Bolan frowned. The voice was familiar. It stirred an echo in his memory. But like the face of the professor in the tavern, he could not place it. He eased up the catch of the grille. There was a heavy metallic click. Very slowly he began to drag back the iron gate. The wheels on their runway shrilled protestingly as the latticework shivered.

"Most vital of all is the shaft," the voice was saying. "We cannot hide the fact that we have sunk a shaft—the pithead gear spells that out for everybody. We shall therefore make a point of showing them that shaft. But we shall conceal the details of its depth. So far as they are concerned it goes no deeper than the lower trial gallery. The elevator is on no account to drop below that level. There is enough there and above to convince them that we are doing what we claim to do. They must not know the full extent of the workings; the fact that we have established a connection between the shaft and the caves is to remain a total secret."

Bolan hauled the gate open another few inches. The opening was now wide enough to allow them through.

Cautiously he peered out. On the grassy slope below the huts, engineers, laborers, overseers and guards were drawn up in front of a raised wooden platform. On it stood a tall, lean man in the uniform of a Soviet admiral. Beside him, addressing the Russians through a bullhorn, was a heavyset man with a shaven skull.

Bolan caught his breath. "Now I've seen it all," he muttered.

"What is it?" Bjornstrom's voice was a whisper.

"That man. His name is Antonin. A KGB colonel. He was one of the top brass, ruthless and cruel. Comrade Antonin and I are old enemies. The fact that he's here makes it all the more urgent to spring Erika."

"How do we know—?"

Bolan laid a finger to his lips. He was scanning the line of huts and the terrain immediately beyond. The huts were clearly sleeping quarters. Behind them rose taller structures—sheds full of excavation equipment, a rock crusher, a glass-roofed mineralogical laboratory. Higher up the slope a wooden mess hall stood by what looked like a headquarters block.

And behind the gantry, half hidden by the shack housing the pithead machinery, a square brick building with the legend in Russian above the door—Chief Overseer. A single guard with a Kalashnikov AKM stood outside at the top of a short flight of steps.

"That's where she is," Bolan murmured.

"Are you certain?"

"Damn right I am. They're putting on a show. Everyone's being told the role they have to play. Only one guy's left to block a doorway. Why would he be there if there wasn't a prisoner inside?"

Bjornstrom nodded. "Guess you're right." He looked at his watch. The minute hand was well past the hour. "She will be waking now."

Swiftly Bolan surveyed the terrain. Antonin was still talking, turning the bullhorn this way and that across the ranks of men before him. The admiral gazed impassively ahead over his folded arms. They were both turned slightly toward the pithead. Beyond them the land dropped away toward the dark water of the fjord. The sunshine, pale but bright, would be directly in their eyes. If Bolan and his companion could steal out of the elevator without attracting their attention and make the shadow between the two nearest huts . . .

The Russian colonel droned on. But the briefing could stop at any minute and the workers disperse to their positions.

Bolan tiptoed toward the bar of shadow.

Bjornstrom followed him out into the sunshine.

The Executioner had estimated that the guard outside the overseer's office would be hidden from Antonin, the sightline blocked by the last hut in the row. From the shadow he saw that he was right.

Bjornstrom joined him between the two huts.

Bolan made his decision. He whispered instructions. Bent low, the two black-suited frogmen figures slipped around behind the huts and sped silently uphill toward the mess hall and the HQ block.

Behind the block they were invisible both to the guard and the assembly below. On a graveled apron in front of the entrance there was a black ZIL limo with diplomatic license plates and a consulate flag above one front fender.

Bolan crawled gingerly over the granite chips until he was level with the front wheels. He raised himself high enough to peer over the top of the hood. Around the corner of the overseer's office, the guard was just visible, perhaps seventy-five or eighty yards away.

At that range the assault rifle would be more accurate.

But Bjornstrom's Ingram was silenced.

Bolan beckoned the Icelander forward. He pointed to the guard and then drew his finger across his own throat. Bjornstrom nodded. He raised the compact SMG.

ERIKA AXELSSON WAS SPREAD-EAGLED naked on a scrubbed wooden table in the back room, her wrists and ankles strapped to the four table legs. She opened her eyes to see two expressionless heavies standing on either side of her. The blue-jowled, balding one held a cheap cigarette lighter in his hand. The blond with pale, red-rimmed eyes poised a surgeon's scalpel as if it was a pen he was about to write with. There was a sheet of typescript in his other hand.

Blue Jowls slapped Erika's face heavily three times. She gasped and jerked away her head, striving to clear her mind from the effects of the drug. Her body ached all over, and there was a burning sensation in one wrist where the strap bit into a sore spot, but otherwise she was undamaged.

"At last," the blond goon grated. "You kept us waiting long enough. Now there's a list of questions you have to answer—" he held up the paper "—but first we are going to hurt you a little to show that we mean what we say, to give you a sample of what will happen to you if you fail to answer correctly."

The girl bit her lip. So this was it. The pill had only brought her a respite. She hoped the zen training she had received would permit her to rise above the pain, the humiliation. She hoped she would be strong enough to resist using the second pill, the cyanide one that could be tongued out of a hollow tooth.

Blue Jowls was leaning over the table, his forearm resting between her spread thighs. "They tell me the singeing of hair is very much the fashion among Western beauty specialists," he said conversationally.

"It can be cut out by the roots," said the man with the scalpel.

"Yeah, but singeing is quicker," Blue Jowls said. He thumbed the lighter into flame.

Erika screamed.

The door burst open.

At first the Norwegian woman did not realize who the two helmeted, rubber-clad figures were. She screamed again when Bjornstrom's hand clamped down to extinguish the smoldering hair at her loins, thinking it some psychological twist in the tormentors' game.

Then she recognized the cold blue eyes and inflexible features of the Executioner.

Bolan sprang for the guy with the scalpel as Bjornstrom whirled to attack Blue Jowls.

The scalpel gleamed wickedly, scything through the air in search of flesh. Bolan dropped to one knee and whipped the commando knife from his boot. The scalpel blade, sharper than ten razors, ripped the sleeve of his wet suit from shoulder to wrist, opening a ten-inch gash in his forearm.

He pivoted on the knee, seizing the torturer's killer arm and pulling it over his shoulder before the guy could attempt a second sweep with the scalpel. The Russian fell forward across Bolan's body.

In the same fluid movement Bolan stabbed viciously upward with the knife. The broad, flat blade sliced through clothing and skin, penetrating the gut.

Bolan twisted and then ripped with all his force.

The Russian uttered a strangled scream and dropped facedown on the floor, the stomach and intestines spilling from his ruptured belly.

Bjornstrom had caught Blue Jowls with a roundhouse right to the side of the head as the hardman tried to pull a Stetchkin automatic from his waistband. Then, as the goon staggered off balance, he swung up the Ingram and jammed the grooved suppressor into his face. The snarling jowls opened to yell, and the fat barrel smashed through teeth to home on the Russian's palate.

Bjornstrom favored the trigger with an instant squeeze.

The triple shot, the splat of blood and brain tissue on the partition wall behind Blue Jowls's head and the smack of .45-caliber bullets tearing through the wood made a single sickly sound. The torturer slid to the floor.

Bolan's knife was slashing the straps that bound Erika to the table.

"You're bleeding!" was all she could gasp as she sat up to rub circulation back into her cramped limbs.

"It's nothing," Bolan said. "A scratch; luckily it didn't go deep." He helped her to stand up, staring at the angry bruises covering her body. "We have to find clothes for you. Sure you're okay?"

"A little sore," she admitted. And then, contriving a grin, she added, "Luckily it didn't go deep."

In a closet in the outer office they found a suit of the now-familiar gray coveralls, a white slicker and a spare pair of boots.

"With your short hair you could pass for one of the overseers at a distance," Bolan said when she had dressed herself. He was binding the wound on his arm with strips torn from a shirt that had been hanging in the closet. "Maybe we could use you to fool them some, once we start shooting."

"Shooting? Are we not getting out?"

He explained the position to her. "It's three-fifteen," he said, glancing again at his watch. "We have to raise hell for at least a quarter hour to make sure they send those kids away."

"But make sure also that we are not still around at four o'clock!" Bjornstrom said.

"Too right," Bolan agreed. "Come on, guys, let's go."

The body of the guard was lying crumpled by the steps outside. Bolan pulled the AKM out from under him. "You know how to use one of these?" he asked the woman. And when she nodded, he simply handed her the gun and said, "Shoot straight, then."

Bjornstrom unclipped two plastic grenades from the man's belt. "These will come in useful also maybe," he said.

They made it to the shadow between the huts opposite the pithead. "We'll cross over behind the shack with the winding mechanism," Bolan decided. "We open up once we're on the far side of the motor pool. We shall be between them and the gates then...with enough ground cover to keep them busy thirty minutes."

"And after that?"

"We'll work that out when we get to it," Bolan said.

Antonin had stopped speaking. The workers and overseers were preparing to disperse to their positions. The shooting would have to start soon, yeah, if it was to be effective enough to have the Russians refuse entry to the professor and his charges.

It started sooner than Bolan expected . . . and not the way he planned.

Bjornstrom had made it to the shack, and he was two-thirds of the way across the sunlit strip with Erika when he saw with horror that the elevator gate was still open.

Whatever else happened it was vital that nobody suspected they had been in the caverns, nobody discovered the dead guards below, nobody started any kind of investigation before those charges went off.

The open grille was a direct giveaway.

Bolan decided it was worth the risk. He would close the grille as far as he could without actually engaging the noisy latch.

He turned to retrace his steps. As the ball of his foot swiveled, a pebble of quartzite crunched loudly. Turning his ankle, he stumbled—and to save himself falling, grabbed instinctively at Erika. His fingers closed around the wrist that had been burned while she was unconscious, and despite herself she gave a cry of pain.

Heads turned along the assembled ranks of Russians. Antonin jerked to attention and stared toward the pithead. For one frozen moment the actors in the drama formed a silent tableau—the Russians astonished, Antonin with the loud-hailer halfway to his mouth, the woman and the helmeted, black-suited intruders, guns in hand, facing the elevator shaft.

The scene exploded into action.

Antonin shouted orders. The guards leaped for their machine pistols, stacked nearly at one side of the parade. Workers fanned out to give them a clear field of fire.

Bolan, figuring that his attitude could mislead the Russians into thinking he and his companions were making for the elevator instead of away from it, sprang back as though he had just opened the grille. And then whirled to race with the woman for the corner of the shack.

"Keep them away from the shaft!" Antonin roared through his bullhorn. "I want them alive if possible, but they're not to make that elevator."

First objective gained, Bolan thought. He dropped down behind a bank of loose dirt in back of the winding-gear shack and brought the Heckler & Koch assault rifle to his shoulder. Erika was kneeling in the shadow cast by the wooden shack, the Kalashnikov aimed toward the huts; Bjornstrom covered the open ground between the huts and the HQ building.

The guards opened fire. From between the huts, behind the baggage trolley, on either side of the platform, Skorpions spat flame. The 700 rpm death stream ripped wood splinters from the walls of the shack and whined off the massive iron spars of the gantry.

Bolan coaxed telling bursts from his G-11, hearing over the deadly rasp of the assault rifle's backfire the deeper reports of Erika's AKM.

A guard fell out from behind the trolley, rolled over in the dust and lay still. Another, caught in the open space between the platform and the huts, sat down abruptly with a hand clasped to his shoulder and blood bubbling between his fingers. The girl downed a man foolish enough to attempt a run between two of the huts.

Antonin and the admiral had disappeared.

The unarmed workers and their overseers were racing for the headquarters block. Each man dashed up the steps and reappeared almost at once with an AKM at port arms.

Bjornstrom dropped several with the silenced Ingram, but the intensity of fire from the guards allowed him only to take rapid snap shots and the final effect was minimal.

With military precision one group circled behind the overseer's office and the rest made for the brow of the hill. Evidently they had orders to outflank Bolan and his companions and attack from the rear.

Guards fired now from the windows of the sleeping quarters. The ironwork of the gantry reverberated with the impact of wasted rounds.

Bolan raked the facades with a lethal stream of the tiny G-11 projectiles. Over the clamor of broken glass he yelled at the Icelander, "Gunnar, try one of the grenades!"

Bjornstrom nodded. His arm swung back. The plastic flesh-shredder arced over the hell ground between the shack and the HQ block to explode with a concussive flash beside the steps. Men fell left and right; a flaming bundle threshed screaming in the doorway.

But the full effect came milliseconds later—three thirty-kilo cylinders of propane gas, ranged outside the block to fuel cooking and heating plant, were blown away from their connecting hoses and erupted with a shattering roar. The explosion smashed a hole in the side of the building and set fire to the interior. A huge fireball blazed upward, drawing after it a column of black smoke.

From behind the row of huts, Antonin's voice, shaking with fury, screamed through the bullhorn, "Azimov, Streletzin—take the Swidnik and head off this damned geologist and his brats. Tell him there was a regrettable accident at the pithead. Tell him anything, but keep the fools away. After that fly back and help us liquidate these terrorists."

Bolan looked across at Bjornstrom and Erika. He held up a thumb. Second objective gained. Following orders—keep the Russians occupied long enough to rule out any checkup of the underground base.

From behind the sheds housing the excavation machinery they heard the whine of a jet engine and then a whir of rotors. The chopper rose into sight, angled through the smoke and flames pouring through the roof of the HQ block and headed for the gates.

Bolan half rose, fired a short burst to discourage any snipers and dashed across to join Bjornstrom and Erika behind the shack. Conserving the remaining G-11 rounds for their eventual getaway, he unleathered Big Thunder. "What we do now—" he began.

Erika screamed a warning.

Bolan whirled. Antonin was standing in the open doorway of the shack. The KGB chief's features were twisted into a manic snarl that was half rage and half triumph. The Tokarev TT-33 in his right hand was aimed point-blank at the Executioner's chest.

Three shots hammered out in a single ragged detonation.

Bolan never knew whether or not it was deliberate, but Gunnar Bjornstrom, hurling himself forward with the Beretta, threw himself into Antonin's path and took the heavy boattail otherwise intended for Bolan.

At the same time Big Thunder blasted a fist-sized hole through the Russian's sternum, and a single round from Erika's AKM sent a 7.62 mm steel-jacket to core his throat.

Antonin died on his feet. He collapsed backward, and the last spurts of his blood turned brown in the dust.

Bolan was bending over the fallen Icelander. "We've got to get him out," he rapped. "Help me carry him to the parking lot."

Behind the nearest vehicle Erika fell to her knees and held Bjornstrom's head in her hands.

"How bad is it?" Bolan asked, firing the AutoMag toward the gantry to keep Russian heads down.

"Bad. Below the right shoulder," she said. "it could be a lung." She held the punctured rubber away from the injured man's flesh. "The suit's filling with blood; I can't stop the flow."

Bolan unwound the makeshift bandage from his arm. The bleeding from the gash had stopped. "Make a pad of that and jam it inside the suit," he said.

Bjornstrom was trying to speak. Bright bubbles of blood foamed at the corner of his mouth as his lips moved. "No good," he whispered. "I cannot make it. Leave me here."

Bolan shook his head. "Take it easy, friend," he said. "We're getting you out of here. In a private ambulance, too!" He raked a glance along the line of parked vehicles.

With a single exception all of them—Zastavas, Skodas, a Moskvitch limo and a Fiat—were parked nose into the bank. The odd man out, an open, jeeplike Pobeda utility, faced the winding dirt road that snaked down the undulating landscape toward the gates.

Bolan vaulted into the driving seat as Erika lowered Bjornstrom as gently as she could into the rear.

No keys hung from the ignition; in fact, there was no ignition switch visible. Bolan glanced swiftly over the dials and tumblers. Nothing. He looked down and saw a push button on the floor behind the central shift lever. He jammed his thumb down on it.

The engine turned, almost caught, coughed . . . and died.

He tried again; once more the engine spun without firing.

"Push!" he yelled to the girl. "But let 'em have it first."

They were protected by the bank, but the Russians had come out into the open and were spreading out to enfilade them. She sprayed them with a blast from the Kalashnikov and they scattered.

Bolan was still leaning vainly on the starter button, but the cold engine obstinately refused to fire. As Erika leaned her shoulder against the Pobeda and rolled it into motion, he slammed it into gear. In a few yards the utility reached a slope leading to the dirt road and began to gather speed under its own weight. Bolan flicked the lever into neutral and coasted.

Erika scrambled aboard and fired another burst.

Behind them now there was shooting—no indiscriminate volleys but single, considered shots. A slug spanged off the Pobeda's body and screeched skyward. The windshield splintered and starred. One of the rear wheels began to thump jarringly as the tire deflated and ran off the rim. They could hear orders through the bullhorn. A truck roared to life.

Bolan clung grimly to the wheel, taking advantage of every irregularity in the track surface to increase their speed. It sounded as if whoever had taken over from Antonin had ordered his men to disable the utility rather than annihilate its occupants.

The final scenario would nevertheless work out as seek-and-destroy. Clearly they could not afford to have anyone at large who had heard the incriminating briefing broadcast by the KGB security chief.

The route, dipping sharply at first, flattened out and then rose to a small crest before it slanted eventually down to the gates. When they were on the steepest part, Bolan wrenched the stick into third gear with the clutch held out, then took his foot off the pedal with a jerk, hoping the engine might catch. There was a whine of gears as the momentum of the car battled against the engine compression...but still no cylinder fired.

The Executioner swore and thrust the lever back into neutral. The utility, which had slowed appreciably, began gathering speed once more. They were out of immediate range now, but there was a truck rocketing after them in a cloud of dust and long lines of men fanning out across the moorland on either side of the trail.

Bolan looked over his shoulder. The Icelander was slumped in a corner, vomiting blood. Erika's face was stricken. In answer to the Executioner's raised brows she shook her head.

Bolan bit his lip. The Pobeda leveled out, sped along the flat stretch and then gradually lost speed as it began the climb toward the crest. When they were still one hundred yards away, it became clear that they were not going to make it.

Cursing again, the warrior bounced in his seat, turning the wheel this way and that, trying to coax the machine further. Erika jumped out and heaved... but the car slowed inexorably, drew to a halt and then started to roll down the hill.

Bolan yanked up on the hand brake and jumped from the car himself. Pausing with his hand on the top rail of the shattered windshield, he saw over the crest the final stretch of track with the closed gates shutting off the outside world...and a mile beyond, far away down the loops of road leading to the highway, the helicopter grounded in front of an elderly bus. Antlike figures milled between the two transports, ancient and modern. And behind, among the huts on the headland, a column of black smoke still stood against the northern sky.

Antonin's emissaries were doing their thing—warning off the kids and their mentor because of a regrettable accident at the mine!

Bolan breathed a sigh of relief. His most pressing problem was solved—the innocent would be out of danger when the charges went off.

The two that remained were serious enough.

Like what was he going to do with Gunnar Bjornstrom? And how was he going to save the woman before the chopper returned to hose death on them from above?

As if he had read the Executioner's thoughts, Bjornstrom himself solved both of them.

Squelching sickeningly in his blood-filled rubber suit, the wounded man dragged himself upright on the seat. His eyes were bright with pain but his voice was firm. "Bolan," he said thickly. "No use. I'm finished and we all know it. Leave me here and I'll hold them off until—"

"No way," Bolan began. "We can't—"

"Please. You must. For Erika." The voice faded and then strengthened again. "Over the crest, there's...gully...a shallow ravine leads down to the valley...where the creek...our boat..."

He stopped speaking, panting for breath.

"Even if we did leave you," Bolan said gently, "they'd get you. You know that. And they mustn't get any of us, dead or alive, because if they could tie in your country, or mine, with this—"

"That's why you must go, both of you," Bjornstrom croaked. "Need you to...carry on fight." He coughed blood. "Anyway I thought of that. They won't get me...not to...identify." He stretched out his unwounded arm and unclenched the fingers of his hand. Lying on his palm was the remaining plastic grenade.

Bolan hesitated. Militarily, it made sense. The truck had screeched to a halt at the foot of the hill, and armed men were running for the cover of boulders strewing the slope of moorland.

"Go," Bjornstrom urged. "Your only chance. You'd never make it...with me. And what's the use? I'm through."

Erika was crying.

"You can put...Ingram across the back of the seat," Bjornstrom said. His voice was weakening now. "Fire one-handed. Leave me one of the pistols. Keep them off for hours...might take a few with me, too." A ghastly smile cracked open his livid features. "Bit of luck for you two, maybe...mine ran out."

Bolan made up his mind. War called for tough decisions. But the mission was more important than individual members of the team, right? And the missions to come.

Besides the guy was right. He was on the way out. It was useless to sacrifice two others for no valid reason.

"Okay," he said crisply, "we'll do that. But take this instead of the Ingram—there should be around fifty rounds left and your own magazine's almost exhausted." He laid the Heckler & Koch assault rifle across the back of the seat and picked up the MAC-11.

Erika slammed a fresh clip into the Beretta and laid it beside the bigger gun. She leaned down to brush her lips against Bjornstrom's forehead and turned away. Her shoulders were shaking.

Bolan held out his hand. "It was a good fight, soldier," he said huskily. "You will be remembered."

The last they saw of the Icelander, before they scrambled up a shallow bank bordering the trail and dropped down on the far side of the crest, he was propped up in the corner of the seat in the sunshine, staring down the dusty road toward the puffs of smoke blossoming from behind the boulders at the foot of the hill. His good hand was curled around the pistol grip of the assault rifle. Erika swore later that he was smiling.

The Russians opened fire on the fugitives as they wormed their way toward Bjornstrom's gully. But there were slabs of granite among the tussocks of coarse grass along the ridge to give them cover.

The Executioner loosed off short bursts from between the rocks until the Ingram's magazine was exhausted. But after that the gunfire from below became sporadic, and only an occasional bullet ricocheted from the outcrops above their heads. Bolan guessed that the KGB killers were advancing up the hill toward the stalled utility.

The warrior and the woman had made the steep, scrub-covered gulch before they heard the first rasp of the Heckler & Kock G-11.

As Bjornstrom had said, the gulch fed into the ravine above the creek, bypassing the edge of the concession. "We have to make that raft pretty damn quick and get it out in the open, in the middle of the fjord," Bolan told her. "They won't dare attack us outside the concession, not even with the chopper, if the boat can be seen from Pvera."

The gully was slippery as well as steep; it would have been impossible to go slowly even if they wanted to. They tumbled, slid and skated down the moss-covered rock bed of the rivulet that ran between its banks until they could see the sunlit waters of the fjord through the thorny branches below them.

It was then that they heard the assault-rifle fire for the second time—one very long burst and then, immediately afterward, a much shorter one. This was followed by an irregular series of lighter shots punctuating the distant reports of the Russian guns.

"Used up all the rounds in the G-11," Bolan muttered. They counted the automatic-pistol shots. Four bursts of three, five single shots, a final triple blast.

And then, shocking in its impact, a savage, cracking detonation that sent echoes clattering from side to side of the ravine and startled flocks of seabirds squawking from the rocks above.

Gunnar Bjornstrom had bowed out the way he wanted it.

The Executioner put an arm around the sobbing woman's shoulders. "Keep going," he said. "He trusted us to take advantage of his courage. If we don't get the hell out of here and carry on the fight we're letting him down."

The raft was in the middle of a fleet of blue-and-white fishing boats, the bus was on its way back to the bridge at the head of the fjord and the helicopter—after a couple of impotent passes over the ravine—had flown back toward the pithead when the first spasm shivered the calm surface of the water.

A mushroom of smoke and dust bellied out from the cliff above the cave mouths, and a huge explosion rolled across the fjord. Before the reverberations of the blast had died away, it was followed by the rumbling roar of thousands of tons of rock collapsing into the water.

The boats rocked crazily as shock waves raced across the surface. One after the other, Bolan sensed rather than heard the muffled minor blasts that would wreck the installations of the secret base now sealed off forever behind the rockfall barring the entrance.

And then, silhouetted against the clear northern sky, the gantry carrying the pithead wheel folded inward and collapsed as a gigantic tongue of flame smashed through the elevator and the shaft erupted in thunderous fury.

When the last rumble had died away and the fishing boats had scattered to take a closer look at the landslide that had tumbled into their fjord, Bolan smiled wearily.

"At least they'll be safe for quite some time from Soviet submarines," he said.

Erika smiled at him, the wide mouth tempting. "And now?" she inquired. "I think you said you *were* on vacation? I'd be happy, very happy to act as your guide and point out some of the more . . . positive . . . pleasures of this country."

Regretfully, he shook his head. The past few days had made the point—vacations were not for him. Not yet. Not while animal man ran wild.

"There will be other bases," he said. "Other submarines. Other fishermen who have the right to live their lives free of fear."

She nodded. There were tears in her eyes. Then she said, "Another time . . . maybe?"

"Maybe," the Executioner said.

**Nile Barrabas and the
Soldiers of Barrabas are the**

by Jack Hild

Nile Barrabas is a nervy son of a bitch who
was the last American soldier out of Vietnam
and the first man into a new kind of action. His
warriors, called the Soldiers of Barrabas, have
one very simple ambition: to do what the
Marines can't or won't do. Join the Barrabas
blitz! Each book hits new heights—this is
brawling at its best!

"Nile Barrabas is one tough SOB himself. . . .
A wealth of detail. . . . SOBs does the job!"
—*West Coast Review of Books*

GOLD
EAGLE

Available wherever paperbacks are sold.

SOBs-1

Take
4 explosive books
plus a
mystery bonus
FREE

Mail to **Gold Eagle Reader Service**

In the U.S.
P.O. Box 1396
Buffalo, N.Y. 14240-1396

In Canada
P.O. Box 2800, Station A
5170 Yonge St.,
Willowdale, Ont. M2N 6J3

YEAH! Rush me 4 free Gold Eagle novels and my free mystery bonus. Then send me 6 brand-new novels every other month as they come off the presses. Bill me at the low price of $2.25 each— a 10% saving off the retail price. There are no shipping, handling or other hidden costs. There is no minimum number of books I must buy. I can always return a shipment and cancel at any time. Even if I never buy another book from Gold Eagle, the 4 free novels and the mystery bonus are mine to keep forever.

Name _____ (PLEASE PRINT) _____

Address _____ Apt. No. _____

City _____ State/Prov. _____ Zip/Postal Code _____

Signature (If under 18, parent or guardian must sign)

This offer is limited to one order per household and not valid to present subscribers. Price is subject to change.

166–BPM–BP6S

4E-SUB-1-R